M000300317

THE
Dragon's
HEART

(Lochguard Highland Dragons #3)

Jessie Donovan

The Dragon's Heart
Copyright © 2016 Laura Hoak-Kagey
Mythical Lake Press, LLC
First Edition

Cover Art by Clarissa Yeo of Yocla Designs.

ISBN 13: 978-1942211426

To all of my older readers

Love isn't reserved solely for the young. May you find your true mate and live happily ever after.

Other Books by Jessie Donovan

Stonefire Dragons
Sacrificed to the Dragon
Seducing the Dragon
Revealing the Dragons
Healed by the Dragon
Reawakening the Dragon
Loved by the Dragon
Surrendering to the Dragon
Cured by the Dragon (October 2016)

Lochguard Highland Dragons
The Dragon's Dilemma
The Dragon Guardian
The Dragon's Heart
The Dragon Warrior (Feb 2017)

Asylums for Magical Threats
Blaze of Secrets
Frozen Desires
Shadow of Temptation
Flare of Promise

Cascade Shifters
Convincing the Cougar
Reclaiming the Wolf
Cougar's First Christmas
Resisting the Cougar

CHAPTER ONE

Lorna MacKenzie eyed her youngest son arguing with flashing dragon eyes and wished for once he'd taken more after his late father, Jamie.

Her inner dragon snorted. *Two serious male sons would've been much worse. Fergus and Fraser balance each other out.*

Fergus and Fraser were Lorna's identical twenty-nine-year-old twins. *I'm not so sure about that.*

Regardless, Fraser does take after Jamie. He's protective.

As she watched her son, Fraser, challenge Ross Anderson, the human male staying with her, Lorna wouldn't disagree with that.

Fraser stood tall, his ginger hair glinting in the light. "I think it's time for you to find your own place, Ross. The cancer's gone and you're taking advantage of my mum's hospitality."

Rather than scold her son for assuming what Lorna wanted, her curiosity wanted to see how Ross would respond.

Her dragon huffed. *And why is that?*

Lorna ignored her beast.

The gray-haired, brown-eyed human male took a step toward Fraser, not the least bit intimidated by the dragonman, who was a little more than thirty-five years his junior. "What I do or who I stay with is none of your concern, lad. If Lorna wanted me to leave, she'd tell me to leave. She's not one to beat around the bush."

"Watch how you speak about my mum, Ross," Fraser growled.

As the two males stared at each other, Fraser's mate and Ross's daughter, Holly, sighed at Lorna's side. "Should we just leave them to have their row? I'd much rather spend time with my baby nephew."

She stopped listening to the two males and answered Holly. "I'm never one to turn down time with wee Jamie, but Fergus needs my help and should be by at any minute."

"Oh?" Holly asked. "What for?"

Lorna smiled. "I can't tell you, child. It's a secret."

Not that Lorna was in on the secret herself. She only knew Fergus wanted her to talk with an old acquaintance. Since Lorna knew everyone in the clan and more than a few secrets about them, she'd help her son with just about anything he needed. She only hoped it was something that could help better protect Clan Lochguard; the attack two months ago still loomed large. It would take many more years to rebuild.

Her dragon grunted. *We've rebuilt before, and we'll rebuild again. Lochguard is strong.*

Aye, we are. But isolation doesn't work as well as it once did. Diplomacy is the future.

Holly opened her mouth to reply to Lorna's statement when Fraser closed the distance between himself and Ross. "Then let me ask her point blank." Fraser looked to Lorna. "So, how about it, Mum? Are you ready to ask this human to leave?"

Holly frowned. "Fraser, that's my dad you're talking about. You shouldn't be so hostile."

Lorna placed a hand on Holly's arm, signaling she'd take care of the situation. "I think you need to go take a dunk in the loch."

10

Fraser blinked. "What?"

From the corner of her eye, she saw Ross trying not to laugh. Clever male. "You heard me. Why you're hell bent on kicking Ross out on his bum, I'll never understand."

"But, Mum, he's more than capable of taking care of himself," Fraser added.

"So? It's only Faye, Ross, and myself here now. I imagine Faye will leave soon, too, and I'd rather not be all by myself in this big house."

It took everything she had not to look at Ross. She and the human got along well. Maybe too well. Lorna had long ago sworn off taking a new mate. Jamie MacKenzie had been her true mate and love of her life. She had vowed never to betray him by taking a new male.

Her dragon huffed. *It's been nearly thirty years. Not even Jamie would've expected us to be alone this long.*

Even if that's true, we're far too old to start dating now. I don't know the first thing to do.

I do. We might be older, but we're not dead. If you're not going to let me fly anytime I want, then you should find a male. Sex will make us both feel good.

Shush, dragon. A friend is all I want.

Maybe soon you'll stop lying to yourself. I know your feelings about him. Why deny it?

She did glance at Ross then. When he met her eye and winked, Lorna's heart skipped a beat. He was attractive, aye, but that wasn't enough for her. If she ever did find the courage to accept another male, she wanted someone to finish growing old with.

And truth be told, Lorna wasn't sure if she was ready to open her heart to another male yet, not even one who could make her laugh or find ways to take away her stress.

Her dragon sighed at the back of her mind. Lorna ignored her beast and focused back on Fraser glaring at her.

She was about to shoo Fraser out of her cottage when the front door opened. Fergus's voiced boomed down the hallway. "Mum? I need you to come with me."

She looked to Fraser, Ross, and back again. "You two either sort yourselves out or separate. When I get back, I want some peace and quiet. If I don't find it, then I will use the wooden spoon on both of your bums."

Without another word, she turned and greeted her other son in the entryway. With the faint sun highlighting his ginger hair and blue eyes, combined with Fergus's calm expression, the lad was the spitting image of his father.

Not wanting to waste time thinking about her dead mate, Lorna raised her brows. "Well? Where are we going?"

"Just come outside. I don't want the others to hear." Fergus raised his voice. "And don't think of spying on me, Fraser."

"Who me?" echoed down the hallway.

Shaking his head, Fergus exited the cottage. Lorna yelled behind her as she followed, "I want silence when I return, or I will smack some bums. I don't give empty threats."

Not wanting to give Ross and Fraser a chance to argue, she shut the door and turned around. Lorna blinked at the male standing on her doorstep. "Stuart MacKay? Is that you?"

The tall dragonman with blue eyes and hair more gray than black smiled. "Lorna Stewart MacKenzie. It's been a while."

She eyed the male she'd known her whole life. "Aye, it has, Stu. But what are you doing here? You're supposed to be with Clan Seahaven."

Seahaven was a small, exiled clan of dragon-shifters with human mates. While the old leader who had exiled them was long gone, the residents of Seahaven had declined moving back to Lochguard. That had prodded Lochguard to try to form an alliance with them. Her son, Fergus, had been facilitating negotiations for months.

Fergus spoke up. "Stuart is Seahaven's representative. We're negotiating a tentative alliance today, but Stuart and his brother, Euan, only agreed to talk if Stuart was allowed to see you during his visit. So, here we are."

Lorna could tell her son didn't think much of the request. Fergus loved efficiency, so he'd see Seahaven's representative chatting with her as nothing more than a waste of time.

Moving her gaze back to Stuart, Lorna eyed the male a year her senior. She hadn't thought about him in a long while, but at one time, they'd been inseparable.

However, her dragon had had other ideas.

Her beast huffed. *Jamie was better.*

Since both Fergus and Stuart still stared at her, Lorna decided to be polite before going in for the kill and demanding more answers.

Lorna kept her tone light as she replied, "That seems a strange deal. But here I am. As you can see, I'm still alive. Not even my devil children have killed me yet."

The corner of Stuart's mouth ticked up. "Not for lack of trying, I bet."

"Hey now, my children adore me." She looked to Fergus and waved. "Tell him."

13

Fergus frowned, but Stuart spoke before he could. "Of course they do. Anyone who knows you would love you, Lorna."

His words set off warning bells in her head. It was best to change the subject. "Now that's sorted, how about we get walking. Then you can tell me all about your mate Deborah and your horde of children."

Sadness flickered in Stuart's eyes. "Deb passed away a few years ago from cancer. And our only son died in his teens at the hands of the dragon hunters."

Bloody hell. Leave it to her to bring up every painful memory in one go. "I'm truly sorry, Stu."

He smiled again. "That means a lot coming from you, Lorna."

Her dragon chimed in. *If you won't go after the human, then what about Stuart?*

Ignoring her beast, Lorna cleared her throat and motioned to their surroundings. "Aye, well, we can chat some more later, and you can tell me all about your braw son and your mate. I lost my own Jamie, so I understand the grief and pain more than most."

Stuart nodded. "I heard about Jamie. I'm sorry, Lorna."

"It was a long time ago." Stuart opened his mouth, but Lorna beat him to it. "But we can talk later. If we don't get a move on, Fergus will have a stroke."

Fergus frowned. "Hyperbole doesn't help anyone."

"Not true. It helps quite a bit with bairns. You'll find that out soon enough, once wee Jamie is walking about and getting into things he shouldn't." A cool breeze blew, and Lorna rubbed her hands together. "For now, it's bloody freezing out here, and we should get moving. My bones aren't a fan of the chill, and I don't think you want to be responsible for my death, Fergus."

Her son sighed at her exaggeration.

However, Stuart grinned at her deliberate use of hyperbole. "Aye, I know the feeling as we're of an age." He put out his arm and waved his elbow. Lorna snorted as she threaded hers through his. Stuart added, "So let's get both of us out of the cold air before we catch our deaths."

Fergus studied them a second. He wisely resisted arguing and merely motioned toward the Protectors' central command. "This way."

As they followed Fergus, Lorna resisted looking up at the handsome, blue-eyed dragonman at her side. While things had been awkward at first, they'd nearly fallen into old times with teasing.

Her dragon spoke up again. *If not Ross, then what about Stuart? Pick one.*

Lorna didn't like ultimatums. And yet, she wondered if maybe she should go after one of the males.

But she would debate all that later. For the moment, she would simply enjoy walking on the arm of a handsome dragonman, especially one she had such a deep history with.

It may have been thirty years, but time wouldn't erase the fact she and Stuart MacKay had nearly mated. If not for Jamie's bold move, her children would've been Stuart's instead.

She wondered exactly why he wanted to see her after all these years. If he was looking for a new mate, then Lorna started to wonder how she would respond.

~~~

Ross Anderson took a deep inhalation and let it out as Fraser and Holly shut the rear door behind them. Ross wasn't usually hotheaded, but Lorna's son had a way of bringing out the worst in him. If his daughter didn't love the bloody dragonman, Ross would've tried long ago to convince her to leave him. But Holly did love him, for whatever reason, so Ross put up with the young lad's overprotectiveness. Well, sometimes. Ross wasn't above taking Fraser by the ear if he ever truly stepped out of line.

Although, Fraser had come close to that line earlier. To be honest, the lad had hit close to home with their row.

Every day Ross wondered if Lorna would ask him to leave. The fact she hadn't done so earlier, when asked point blank, made him think he might still have a chance with the dragonwoman.

He well knew Lorna mourned her dead husband still. Ross understood the feeling better than anyone considering his own wife had been murdered over a decade ago. Much like Lorna loved her dead husband, he'd always love Anne. Truth be told, Ross had never expected to find someone else, especially once the cancer had taken hold.

But the treatments his daughter had given up so much for had worked. A few weeks ago, he'd been declared cancer-free. For the first time in a long time, he had a future.

And while Lorna may be determined to keep her heart closed off, Ross wanted more than their chats or head shaking over their children. Not just because she was beautiful—although she was to him—but also because of her heart, vivaciousness, and humor. He could see them growing old together. Or, rather, older together.

Only because it was illegal for human males and female dragon-shifters to mate had he kept his feelings about Lorna a secret and delayed his plans to pursue her. Well, secret might not be the right word. But if the laws had been different, he would've coaxed a kiss from the fiery woman the day he'd learned his cancer was gone.

And yet, with the recent mating on the telly between a female dragon-shifter named Nikki Gray and a human male named Rafe Hartley, Ross was starting to think he might have a chance with Lorna MacKenzie.

Right, Anderson. The longer you put it off, the greater the chance someone else will steal her away. As it were, he was surprised Lorna didn't have a horde of men after her. Probably because the bloody woman only seemed concerned with taking care of everyone else and never herself.

That would soon change if Ross had anything to say about it. After Lorna helping him for so many months, he wanted to repay the favor and then some.

Just thinking of holding Lorna close and kissing her caused heat to rush through his body. He'd spent many a night dreaming of the woman.

It was time to make those dreams a reality.

He just needed to think of a plan. Sitting in the chair in the front room, Ross tried to think of how to get some alone time with the dragonwoman when he spotted Lorna walking away on the arm of a tall man through the window. The man turned his head with a smile. The bloke was too old and gray to be her son.

While Ross didn't know everyone on Lochguard as well as most, he couldn't recall ever seeing the man.

His heart skipped a beat. Maybe he'd been a daft fool and waited too long after all.

No. He wasn't about to give up until he knew more. The other man leaning down to smile at Lorna might be a friend or even a relative. Ross wouldn't think the worst.

17

He would find a way to be alone with Lorna this evening and find out all he could. If there was even a sliver of a chance, Ross would pull out all the stops to convince the stubborn woman to give him a chance.

Lorna had spent decades raising her children and looking out for them. With them all grown, it was high time she had some pleasure for herself. And Ross was going to be the one to give it to her.

CHAPTER TWO

A silence lulled as Lorna walked with Stuart MacKay and she decided she was done with pleasantries. "Why did you volunteer to come to Lochguard?"

Stuart raised his brows. "You don't want peace between our clans?"

"Aye, of course I do. However, Fergus and Finn are in charge of the negotiations, not me. I want to know why you wanted to see me specifically."

He winked. "You always did get straight to the point."

"Of course. It saves a lot of time. Clan leaders would get twice as much done if they only spoke their minds." She pulled gently on his arm. "So, why?"

Stuart looked to Fergus slightly ahead of them and back to her. He leaned down to whisper into her ear, "We were friends once, Lorna. I'd like to be friends again. So when I heard my brother was looking for a go-between for Lochguard, I volunteered." He leaned closer and his hot breath tickled her ear. "As far as I hear it, you're unattached."

Not caring if Fergus heard or not, she replied, "That isn't any of your bloody business."

"Ah, so there is someone."

She hesitated. Ross had come close to kissing her a few times during his stay on Lochguard, but he had never seen it through. Every time she'd accepted that they'd only be friends, the blasted male would take her hand, and a sizzle would travel up her spine, confusing her.

Her beast spoke up. *There's nothing saying you can't be the one to kiss him. Times are different now.*

Ignoring her dragon, she tried to think of how to reply to Stuart's supposition. She could say yes and drive him away. On the other hand, if Ross fancied someone else, it would be nice to have someone to talk to. After all, she and Stuart had been close once.

She wanted to slap her cheeks. For nearly thirty years, she'd never once thought about pursuing another male. And yet there she was, thinking about two in a day.

Goodness gracious, she wasn't much better than a teenager.

Clearing her throat, she answered, "You focus on your meeting and negotiations and we can talk later."

Determination flashed in Stuart's eyes. Maybe he'd taken it as encouragement.

Stuart nodded. "I look forward to that."

Lorna had no idea if Fergus had heard her conversation with Stuart or not, but her son never turned around to interject. Unlike Fraser, Fergus knew how to hold his tongue. Well, unless his mate or family's lives were at stake. Then all bets were off.

The lad was more like his father than he'd ever know.

They arrived at one of the entrances to the Protectors' central command. Unless she wanted gossip to spread like wildfire and reach Meg Boyd's—her friend but also rival's—ears, it looked like Lorna would have to continue her conversation with Stuart later.

Her dragon spoke up. *It also gives me time to change your mind. Who says I've made up my mind?*

THE DRAGON'S HEART

Interesting. You've sworn off males and love for nearly thirty years. Maybe Stu is what you were waiting for? The human would bring risk, but a dragon-shifter would be safe.

At one time, Lorna might've thought that about Stuart MacKay. When she'd kissed Jamie MacKenzie and fallen into the mate-claim frenzy, she'd cared about him but hadn't yet loved him. It hadn't taken long for her auburn-haired dragonman to win her heart, but for a brief amount of time, she hadn't ruled out going back to Stuart if Jamie didn't work out. All dragon-shifters had the right to refuse their true mate if they didn't fit well. While fate usually did a bang up job, there were always cases when it didn't work out. Some clans might force it, but in recent history, Lochguard hadn't been one of them and still wasn't.

Yet, as she looked at Stuart from the corner of her eye, Lorna had to admit he'd aged well. The laugh lines around his mouth and crinkles at the corner of his eyes only added to his appeal.

Of course, Ross had a dimple in one of his cheeks when he smiled. And his brown eyes were more like whiskey than chocolate.

Her dragon huffed. *Then go after Ross. He wants us.*

What are you talking about? Ross has never once moved to woo me. Every time I thought he'd kiss me, he backed off. We get along. That's it.

For such a clever female, you're missing something.

She mentally rolled her eyes. *And what's that, you oh-so-clever beast?*

Until a few weeks ago, Ross didn't know if he had a future. Now that he's cancer-free, he does. You saw the look in his eyes earlier when you didn't order him out. He fancies us.

Lorna nearly missed her step and her dragon laughed before adding, *You know it's true. The question now is, do you want Ross or Stu?*

She dismissed the choice as ridiculous since Lorna didn't need a male in her life to complicate things when they reached the meeting room. She forced herself to pay attention to her son and the current negotiations. Her silly male problems could wait.

Her dragon merely sat at the back of her mind with a smug expression.

Lorna would deal with that headache later.

Once Fergus shut the door to the private conference room, they all sat down around the table before he spoke up. "Right, then. Let's go over the points of our latest agreement and see if we can't get it signed."

As Lorna watched her son and her former lover discuss an alliance, she wondered what she'd do if her dragon was correct about Ross and Stuart. For the most part, the males on Lochguard knew she wasn't interested. But Ross, and even Stuart, didn't fit those parameters.

The real question was whether she wanted a new mate or not.

Lorna knew the answer but was afraid to admit it. While Jamie taking her away from Stuart had been bad enough, Lorna now had her children and nephew to worry about. They were all grown and protective of her. It was sweet, considering Lorna could take care of herself. But it was only a matter of time before their protective Stewart and MacKenzie genes kicked into overdrive. The last thing Lochguard needed was drama, let alone dragons challenging each other in the sky. Fergus might restrain himself, but Fraser and Faye most definitely would not.

Her dragon chuckled. *Then you are going to pick one. I can't wait.*

The Dragon's Heart

Lorna resisted a sigh. She might have a few battles coming to her. The question was whether she looked forward to it or dreaded it.

Or, was it a bit of both?

~~~

Later in the day, as the sun moved lower in the sky, Ross picked up a twig from the ground and twirled it in his fingers. He hoped Lorna would come.

He'd left a note for her to meet him in one of the hidden clearings toward the back of the clan. Ross had spent every afternoon walking around Lochguard as part of his recovery and had stumbled upon the clearing by mistake.

It was a wide-open space, with trees ringing the edge. If ever there was a place he could convince Lorna to shift for him and only him, it was here.

He only hoped he wasn't being daft, especially since the air was still chilly in early April and his joints didn't tolerate the cold as they once had. The only saving grace was that it wasn't raining, or he would have to postpone, which he wanted to avoid at all cost. He'd made his decision, and Ross intended to see his plan through.

He knew that unless Lorna shared both halves of herself with him, they would never have a shot at a future together. He needed to see Lorna in dragon form.

He was also determined to find out whatever she was hiding because he was positive she was afraid of something.

He paced back and forth. He wasn't fond of the whole text messaging trend, so he'd written a letter and left it for her in the kitchen. Ross hoped she had found it, or he'd be waiting a long time.

Glancing at his watch, Ross noted that Lorna had three minutes before she'd be late. The closeness worried him since Lorna was punctual to a fault.

However, he heard someone pushing through the underbrush. Looking up, he spotted Lorna walking toward him with a curious expression.

Despite being wrapped in a big coat, the combination of the wind gently blowing her graying blonde hair and the flush on her cheeks sent a rush of heat through his body. Before he could think too hard about it, he blurted out, "You're beautiful."

Lorna frowned as she stopped a few feet from him. "Pardon?"

Ross's heart beat double-time inside his chest. It'd been a long while since he'd had to woo a lass, but he wasn't going to let that stop him. "With you always going on about how keen your hearing is, I know you heard me, woman. You're beautiful."

Lorna searched his eyes before answering, "Aye, I heard it the first time. But I'm wondering why you said it."

Taking a few steps closer, he reached out and tucked a section of hair behind her ear. Lorna drew in a breath, and he smiled. "That's what I thought."

She took a step back. "I don't know what you're talking about, Ross Anderson. You left me a cryptic message to meet you in the middle of a blasted clearing. Why am I here?"

"Because," he answered as he closed the distance again, "I want to see you shift."

Lorna tried to move away again, but Ross reached out and pulled her up against his body. As he stared into her eyes, uncertainty flashed. Considering how strong of a woman Lorna was, Ross didn't like it.

Lorna spoke up before he could speak again. "I've told you once, and I'll tell you again—I don't shift much anymore. My old bones can't take it."

Her pupils flashed to slits and back. A corner of Ross's mouth ticked up. "I think your dragon is already calling you a liar."

"So you speak dragon now?"

"Don't be silly, Lorna. But what else could your dragon be saying? Especially since all the other clan members our age shift all the time." He moved a hand to her back and stroked. He waited to see if she'd still or pull away, but Lorna's expression didn't change. It gave him the encouragement to keep pushing. "I want to know why you keep dismissing it. You rarely ever lie that I'm aware of. So, why are you afraid of showing me your dragon, Lorna MacKenzie? Is it because I'm human?"

Her brows furrowed again. "Of course not. Being human or dragon doesn't influence my opinion one way or the other."

"Then what it is?"

After holding his gaze a second, she sighed. "You aren't going to let me go unless I shift, are you?"

"No," he answered with a grin.

"You do remember that I'm stronger than you, right?"

He growled and moved his head closer. "We've long established you're stronger than me with better hearing and eyesight. You don't have to keep kicking a man down."

Snorting, Lorna patted his chest. "But it's so much fun."

Moving his hand from her back to her cheek, he murmured, "I can think of something else that's fun."

Desire mixed with confusion filled Lorna's eyes. "You're being cryptic again."

"Then let me show you, woman."

25

Before she could push him away or reply, Ross lowered his head and kissed her.

~~~

Lorna had been arguing with her dragon when Ross finally kissed her.

She half-expected for guilt and betrayal to course through her body, but as her human's lips touched hers, a yearning long buried rushed forth.

It was desire.

Ross was gentle at first, but the instant she leaned against him and threaded her fingers through his hair, he grew bolder and slid his tongue into her mouth.

Each hot, firm stroke stirred both woman and beast. It'd been far too long since she'd been kissed by a male.

Her dragon growled. *Then start kissing him back.*

Lorna wasn't sure if she remembered how to kiss a male properly, but decided what the hell, and met Ross's tongue stroke for stroke. As he groaned into her mouth and pressed her closer against his body, she couldn't miss his erection pressing against her belly.

Her dragon hummed. *Yes, yes. After all this time, we can have sex again.*

Her dragon's words sent a thread of shyness through her body. Lorna MacKenzie might be brash and able to handle her unruly brood, but she was most definitely not a sexual goddess.

Ross must've sensed her thoughts because he broke the kiss and murmured, "What's wrong, Lorna?"

Since her hand remained threaded through Ross's hair, she gently stroked his scalp. The motion helped her to focus her thoughts. She decided to tell him the truth. "It's been a long time, Ross. And I'm not as young as I once was. Even for a dragon-shifter, birthing and raising three children takes a toll on a female."

He snorted. "You really don't know how lovely you are, do you?" He traced the lines around her mouth and eyes. "Each one of these represents a story and at least a dozen memories. I much prefer my women with personality and a history over fake beauty any day."

She studied him. "I can't tell if you're sweet-talking me or being serious."

He rolled his eyes. "I'm not exactly the sweet-talking type of man when it comes to you, Lorna. After all these months together, I thought you'd realize that by now."

Lightly slapping his chest, she replied, "It all came on a bit suddenly, you devil. After all these months, why now?"

Searching her eyes, Ross answered, "Until my cancer was gone, my hands were tied. I didn't want you to grow close to someone only to have them ripped from your side again, lass."

"Like Jamie."

"Aye, like your mate Jamie." He paused a second to take her chin in hand. "Tell me about him." She opened her mouth to protest, but he cut her off. "And don't dismiss it. It's clear as day you still think of him often, as you should. But not talking about him means you can't share your love with the world."

She looked at him askance. "Since when did you become so wise?"

"I have my moments," he said with a wink.

Lorna chuckled. "You must've been quite the charmer with the lasses when you were younger."

"Aye, I was, and I'd like to think I still am. But it was a quiet woman who eventually caught my eye. However, we're not talking about Anne until you tell me about Jamie."

Jamie. Just remembering his final smile as he'd rubbed her pregnant belly twisted her heart. "He was a fool."

"Pardon?"

She looked up again. "It's true. I loved him more than life itself, but rather than wait out a lightning storm, he charged home the second he heard I was in labor.

"He said he'd seen his first two children born and wouldn't deprive the youngest of his presence, or he'd never hear the end of it whilst the girl was growing up."

Ross smiled. "Knowing Faye as I do, she probably would've brought it up all the time."

"Aye, she would have." Her throat closed up, and her voice cracked. "But if he'd waited for an hour or two, the storm would've passed, and he still would've made it home in time. The idiot."

Her dragon rumbled, *No one can change the past. You know that. It still doesn't mean I can't wish for it to be different.*

Gathering her close, Ross laid his cheek on top of her head. His warm presence comforted her. "Even with him gone, you know he loved you and the bairns." Ross paused, stroking her back. "My demon is that I could've done more to protect my wife, and I didn't do it."

~~~

Ross may have accepted his late wife was gone, but the guilt sat heavily on his shoulders.

For Holly's sake, he'd hidden it deep inside. His Holly-berry had been distraught enough with the news of her mother's murder. She didn't need a remorseful and grieving father to add to her troubles.

He'd never really talked about his guilt. And yet, he knew Lorna well enough to know she wouldn't push him away and run for the hills. She'd hear everything before making a decision.

Speaking of Lorna, she pulled back and met his gaze again. "I somehow think you're inflating the situation, human."

He raised his brows. "So you dug into my past, did you?"

"Of course not. But given how protective you and Holly are of each other, I can't imagine you failing your late female on purpose."

He shook his head. "Anne feared for her life toward the end, what with that man stalking her. I couldn't make the bloody police see the threat and take it seriously. Only when it was too late, and Anne had been murdered did they look into it." He moved a hand to run through his hair. "I could've moved to a different city to protect my wife. But I had been more concerned about an upcoming promotion and worried about our finances. It all seems ridiculous in retrospect."

"Your female was murdered by an obsessive stalker, aye? I somehow doubt he would've given up easily. Unless you moved to America or some other far off location, he would've found you."

"I don't know about that," Ross said. "He probably wouldn't have trekked to rural Wales to find her."

Lorna clicked her tongue. "In this day and age, even back when your wife was taken from you, it's easy enough to find people with the internet. You would have to change your name and maybe even your appearance to truly disappear. Few can manage that without the government's help."

He shook his head. "I refuse to believe there was nothing we could've done."

"Listen to me, Ross Anderson. I know the game of what-ifs better than anyone. I could've told Jamie to stay away, or I'd kick him out of the cottage. Or, I could've had the doctor convince him I had plenty of time before I would give birth. But I did none of those things. Would he still have flown back in the storm? Maybe, maybe not. But I'm sixty years old and like to think I have some wisdom. Time machines don't exist, and that's the only true way a person could change the past."

Ross tilted his head. "I call bullshit."

Lorna clicked her tongue. "Watch yourself, Ross. Even without shifting, I can extend a talon or two. You don't want to upset me."

"You're acting as if I'm the unreasonable one, yet you won't even bloody shift into a dragon even though that's half of who you are. I think it's related to Jamie's death, which means you haven't accepted the past as much as you would like me to believe." Lorna hesitated, and he decided to push. "You want to convince me differently? Then shift and prove you've moved on. Then you can start lecturing me about my own guilt."

Lorna searched his eyes. "I'm not sure I like how you're trying to manipulate me, Ross Anderson. I'm smarter than that."

"Oh, I know you're clever. But it doesn't mean that I won't try."

With a snort, Lorna pushed against his chest. "As long as you know you can't win against me."

He raised his brows. "Oh, aye? I think I have a few tricks to prove you otherwise. Shift, my dear, and you'll find out before long. I may even have you begging."

30

THE DRAGON'S HEART

As Lorna's pupils flashed, Ross resisted a smile. He'd like to think her beast was on his side. From what he'd gleaned from his time on Lochguard, the dragon halves were extremely sexual. Lorna may be older and out of practice, but Ross was confident that as soon as he had her naked and to himself, Lorna would be a firecracker. Her dragon would only make her more so.

She raised her chin. "I'll shift, but first, I want another kiss. And not just a peck on the cheek either, but one to please my dragon."

Grinning, Ross cupped her cheek. "I knew you couldn't resist my charms, lass."

Lorna rolled her eyes. "I could do without the cockiness."

"Aye, maybe you could. But I like to think it adds to my appeal."

"Hurry up and kiss me, you old fool, or I'll rescind my offer."

Leaning down, Ross murmured, "We can't have that, now, can we?" He nipped her bottom lip. "Brace yourself, love. Your dragon is going to like this."

Taking Lorna's lips in a rough kiss, Ross wrapped his free arm around her waist and pulled her closer. He explored her mouth, taking in her taste and heat. Lorna was sunshine mixed with cream.

He took the kiss deeper, stroking possessively against her tongue. No matter how long it took, he'd keep kissing her to please her dragon. And then maybe a wee bit longer for himself.

CHAPTER THREE

Lorna allowed Ross to dominate her mouth for a moment before she pushed back and battled his tongue.

The human sure knew how to kiss. Not that she'd ever tell him. It would go straight to his head.

Her dragon spoke up. *Stop thinking and just enjoy it. Our human clearly desires us.*

Ignoring her beast's words about their human, Lorna ran a hand down Ross's back to his bum cheek. He squeaked a second before growling into her mouth. The vibration sent a thrill through her body, straight between her legs.

Her dragon chimed in again. *Yes, yes. I want more.*

Not now. Things are complicated.

How? You want him. He clearly wants us. Take him.

Ross broke the kiss to murmur, "Stop thinking so hard, woman."

"Don't tell me—"

But Ross interrupted her with another kiss. Both human and dragon halves liked this new side to Ross.

Moving his hands from her face to her back, Ross cupped her rear and rocked her against his erection. Lorna gasped at the contact.

Ross chuckled. "Just wait until you see me in all my glory, lass. Then you really will gasp."

"I call bullcrap."

"Oh, aye? Then maybe we should settle this once and for all. It's a wee bit chilly out, but I'm sure we can find somewhere to put this to rest."

She tried not to smile. "I'm not about to canoodle in an abandoned cottage, Ross. You might break your hip."

He nipped her bottom lip. "Cheeky wench."

Chuckling, Lorna leaned down to lick the skin of his neck. "For that, I should let my dragon out. She'll demand some gymnastic-level maneuvers and then I can laugh when you do break your hip, old man."

Ross leaned back until he could meet her gaze. "As much as I want to try that, I think it's time to show me your dragon form, Lorna. Because there won't be any more kisses until you do."

She raised her brows. "I've survived years without kisses. I'm not sure if that's much of a threat."

Her beast huffed. *But I want more kisses. And much more. Let's just shift and show him. We don't have to fly.*

Lorna hesitated. She hadn't stood before a male unrelated to her and shifted since her Jamie had passed. The act would almost be a final good-bye. Lorna wasn't sure if she was ready for that.

Her dragon's voice was soft when she said, *Jamie will always be with us. He would want us to be happy. Ross might finally be able to give us that. Then we'd never be lonely again.*

As much as Lorna loved her children and her nephew, there had been many nights when she'd needed the warm embrace and soothing words of a mate. She'd always thought it would never happen, but when Ross kissed her, argued with her, or even teased her, it all just felt... right.

33

Ross's voice interrupted her thoughts. "We're too old to hesitate, my dear. I might keel over in the next minute. So, what's it to be?"

"You're not going to keel over anytime soon."

"Aye? So, you can predict the future now?"

"You're incorrigible."

Ross grinned and then winked at her. His dimple came out and weakened her resolve a fraction. He replied, "So, what's it to be? I know my kisses are pretty spectacular, so I'm leaning toward you shifting."

She rolled her eyes. "At this rate, I wouldn't be surprised if I sprain a muscle rolling my eyes since you make me do it so often." He lightly pinched her bum and Lorna squeaked. "That was uncalled for."

"We can talk about how you liked it later. Right now, I want to see your dragon, my dear. So, what will it be? I let you go and you walk away. Or, you shift and then receive more kisses from me once you're human again."

The corner of her mouth twitched. "I'm almost tempted to say you need to kiss my dragon's snout before you get any more kisses from my human form. I'm fairly certain your cockiness would fade when I flashed my long, sharp teeth."

"Stop stalling and make your decision. If I wait any longer, I might lose all my hair."

A retort was on the tip of her tongue, but her dragon spoke up again. *Enough with the human games. Let's shift and then I can play with him.*

At the image of her beast dangling Ross in the air, Lorna mentally chuckled. *Aye, I'd like to see that.*

Then let's shift.

What the hell. It's only Ross.

The Dragon's Heart

She pushed against the human's chest, and he released her. Lorna walked about ten feet away. "Turn around."

Crossing his arms across his chest, Ross smiled. "I'd rather not. Besides, I thought dragon-shifters didn't care about nudity."

He was right, the blasted human. Yet having Ross's single-minded attention, as his gaze raked from her head to her toes, caused her heart to beat double-time.

Rather than admit she was nervous, Lorna drew on her formidable strength and unzipped her coat. "Fine, but if I hear so much as a chuckle or see a look of horror, I'm going to lift you into the air and drop you into the freezing loch."

He motioned with his hand. "Understood. Now, get to it, woman. Show me your beautiful dragon."

Ross's words rang with honesty, not fake platitudes. Combined with the warmth and anticipation in his eyes, Lorna kicked off her shoes. "Right, then stand back."

It was time to show Ross Anderson her dragon form.

~~~

Ross couldn't stop smiling. After all these months, Lorna was finally going to share her dragon with him.

Of course, he didn't think too much more on it as the woman tossed aside her jacket and moved her hands to the bottom of her jumper.

With a twinkle in her eye, Lorna raised the jumper inch by inch, slowly revealing the pale skin of her abdomen. Just as she would expose her breasts, she paused. "Are you sure you can survive this? I don't want to give you a heart attack."

He grinned. "It will be a hell of a way to die."

Sighing, Lorna muttered something he couldn't hear, apart from the last bit of him being "a pervy old human."

He half expected her to stop and change her mind. Or, at the very least, to tell him to turn around. But something flashed in Lorna's eyes and she tugged her jumper off in one swift motion. Her large breasts were encased in a black, lacy bra. He itched to touch them and feel their weight in his hands. But since he didn't want to scare the dragonwoman off, he met Lorna's eyes and chuckled. "Look who has fancy underthings."

Placing her hands on her hips, Lorna raised her brows. "There's nothing wrong with wearing things to make me feel pretty."

"Love, you could be wearing nothing and still outshine the stars." At the skepticism in Lorna's eyes, Ross added, "Why are you stalling? You're the one always complaining about the cold. The sooner you're naked, the sooner you can shift into a dragon. Dragon's don't feel the cold as keenly, or so your children say."

Lorna said nothing for a few seconds, and he wondered if he had said too much. Then the dragonwoman wiggled out of her stretchy leggings. Ross drank in every curve and valley of her form. "Lovely."

Rather than reply, Lorna shucked her panties. Lorna hooked a finger under her bra, and Ross licked his lips. He'd spent many a night dreaming about those breasts.

Whatever shyness Lorna had possessed in the beginning was nowhere to be found as she slowly lowered one bra strap and then the other. Reaching behind her, Lorna smiled right before her bra fell to the ground. Ross's mouth watered. Lorna's plump skin was topped with pointy nipples. He couldn't wait to take one into his mouth.

Lorna cleared her throat. "My face is up here, Ross."

With one last look, he met Lorna's whiskey-colored eyes. Her pupils flashed to slits and back. His voice was husky to his own ears as he replied, "I've had months to memorize your face, Lorna. From the slight tilt of your left eyebrow to the mole near your jaw. I may need a few months to similarly memorize the soft skin of your breasts, your abdomen, and that lovely arse of yours."

Lorna's cheeks flushed, and Ross's ego went up a notch.

In the next second, Lorna's skin glowed a faint green before her nose elongated into a snout, wings sprouted from her back, and her form stretched to a height over ten feet.

Ross barely had time to shut his dropped jaw before Lorna stood in the clearing in her green dragon form. As if wanting to add a little drama, she flicked her wings up and out. The wingspan had to be more than twenty feet.

As he continued to stare, Lorna shook her head, and it broke the spell.

Not wanting Lorna to change her mind and shift back, Ross walked slowly to her side. He moved his hand until it was an inch from her green-scaled side and met her large dragon eye. "I just want to make sure you're not going to bite me if I pet you."

After she flashed a grin, Lorna's chest rumbled with what he assumed was a dragon chuckle.

The question had been more out of curiosity, but it seemed to have broken the tension. Ross gently ran a hand down Lorna's side. The green, grooved scales were sleek but tough like hardened leather.

He kept his hand on Lorna's side as he moved down her body. Once he stood under an outstretched wing, he reached up, but couldn't quite make contact with the bat-like appendage. Lorna lowered her wing until he could lightly brush the thinner membrane between her wing bones. While tough, the skin was softer than her scales.

Chancing a glance over his shoulder, he found Lorna watching him with curiosity. The dragonwoman was trying to hide it, but the tension of her body told him she was nervous. He needed to make her feel more at ease. "Don't try to hurry me, woman. You'll learn to appreciate my attention to detail later on. Believe me, I like to investigate every inch of your woman form. Maybe even with my tongue."

Heat flashed in Lorna's dragon eyes, and Ross resisted a chuckle. He didn't want to push her too far.

He reluctantly lowered his arm and continued down her body to her tail. Lorna flicked it at him but stopped a few inches before it would hit him in the bollocks. At the sound of another dragon chuckle, he frowned and looked over his shoulder. "Smacking me there would be quite the loss for you, lass. Besides, we don't want to risk breaking my old hip, now do we?"

He winked and Lorna shook her head. Ross could just imagine what the woman wanted to say.

Just as he stepped over her tail, Lorna wrapped the long appendage around his waist. She lifted him into the air and rotated until he was upside down. With a gentle shake, his keys and wallet fell out.

But he couldn't be cross at the amusement dancing in Lorna's eyes. He bet it'd been years since she'd played with anyone in her dragon form.

He still couldn't believe she was sharing it with him.

A second later, he was back on his feet, and she released him. Ross moved to her head and petted Lorna's snout. As he stared at the lovely green dragon in the late afternoon light, Ross murmured, "Thank you for sharing your dragon with me."

THE DRAGON'S HEART

~~~

Lorna was on the verge of tears. The usually stubborn, opinionated Ross Anderson was being kind and gentle. He'd even smiled as she dangled him from her tail.

For years, Lorna had wondered what she'd feel if she ever shared her dragon with a male she cared for. Would she feel guilty? Shy? Or, even angry for betraying her dead mate? Yet as she gazed into Ross's eyes, it seemed all of her worries had been unfounded.

Her beast spoke up. *Of course they were.*

I needed the time to heal, dragon. Jamie was our true mate; it wasn't easy getting over him.

I know, but you just needed the right male to share it with.

Eyeing Ross as he continued to pat her nose, Lorna knew her beast was right. Seeing Stuart earlier had been nice, but the mere thought of shifting into a dragon and flying in the air with him made her stomach twist. Maybe Ross was what she needed. Being human, he was different from Jamie. That made it easier.

Her dragon huffed. *Whatever the reason, it's now time to coax him into bed.*

Not yet.

Why not? You know him well. He's attractive and likes us. What else is there?

The children.

Her dragon grunted. *Fraser might never accept it.*

Regardless, I need to talk with them before I make any long-term plans.

Fine. But there's no harm in a little more kissing, now, is there?

Lorna didn't disagree. Gently wrapping her talons around Ross's middle, she lifted and placed him as far as she could reach.

39

When she released him, she put up a paw. Ross nodded. "Aye, I understand. While you shift, I'll fetch your clothes."

As the handsome, mature human scrambled to pick up her discarded clothing, warmth tugged at her heart. Ross may not be a dragon-shifter, but he still would look after his female.

The only question was whether Lorna would find the balance between him and her children. As much as she cared for Ross, her children would always come first.

Imagining her snout shrinking, her wings morphing into her back, and her talons retreating to fingernails, Lorna decided she'd find out sooner rather than later.

Standing in the chilly air, Lorna wrapped her arms around her body. Ross rushed forth and wrapped her coat around her shoulders before running his hands to her lower back under the material and pulling her close. She tried to narrow her eyes but failed. "Someone has wandering hands."

Grinning, Ross gently squeezed her waist. "And you say that like it's a bad thing."

"My breasts are off limits, for now, Anderson. Try it, and see what happens."

Ross chuckled. "We'll save those beauties for later." Nuzzling her cheek, he murmured, "But I'm impatient for another kiss."

Between his heat and scent, Lorna wanted nothing more than to curl up against him and revel in his long arms around her. But before she could do that, she needed a MacKenzie family meeting.

However, she tilted her head toward Ross and whispered, "Just one and then we need to head back. Everyone is due for dinner soon, and you know what happens when the MacKenzie horde doesn't eat on time."

"Aye, all hell breaks loose."

She lightly slapped his chest. "That is my family you're talking about."

"They are, but I say it with love."

She snorted. "Right, if you say so. I might just take back my request for a kiss."

"No bloody way I'm allowing that to happen," Ross growled before taking her lips in a rough kiss.

Lorna sighed at his touch and welcomed his tongue. The human didn't hesitate before dominating her mouth.

Her dragon spoke up. *Just imagine what else he can do with that tongue.*

Pervy dragon.

That's what happens after so many years of celibacy. When can we have him? All of him?

Maybe tonight. I'll talk to the kids at dinner.

Before her dragon could reply, Ross moved a hand to her left arse cheek and squeezed. Lorna moaned as she pulled Ross closer.

Now that she'd overcome her fear and guilt, Lorna was nearly as impatient as her dragon to get her human naked and above her.

CHAPTER FOUR

Once Lorna was dressed again, Ross threaded his fingers through hers. He waited to see if she would pull away or if she'd allow him to make such a claim in front of the clan.

She looked down at their clasped hands and then met his gaze. Raising her brows, she asked, "Make very certain of this, Ross. Not everyone is going to welcome you with open arms. They may have tolerated you during your recovery and because of Holly, but stealing away one of their females is quite different."

"Are you talking about that bloke from this morning?"

Lorna blinked. "You saw that?"

"Aye, I did. Who is he?"

"Well, his name is Stuart MacKay and once upon a time, I was going to mate him."

Ross frowned. "Before or after Jamie?"

"Before. I dated Stu for about a year before I even noticed Jamie. Stu and I had an argument, and shortly after, Jamie snuck a kiss from me at a gathering. I hadn't thought anything about it at the time and rather thought kissing someone else would convince me to give Stu another chance. However, the kiss started the mate-claim frenzy."

Squeezing Lorna's fingers, he asked, "So you weren't in love with Jamie MacKenzie at first?"

She shook her head. "No. I fancied him a bit, but the love came later. Stu didn't take it well but left me alone because I was carrying Jamie's child. Or, rather, as we found out later, the twins." She smiled at him. "Eventually, Stu found his own mate with a human female. The old leader kicked him out of the clan because of his human mate. He and his brother, Euan, helped to found Clan Seahaven."

"That's why I haven't seen him before."

"Aye. He surprised me this morning, but apparently, he's acting as Seahaven's representative and negotiating with Fergus."

"He'd better not have made courting you part of the negotiations," Ross growled.

"Don't be ridiculous. Stu, and pretty much every Scottish dragon-shifter, knows that wouldn't fly with me. You should know that too, Anderson. If not, then maybe I should rethink kissing you again."

Tugging her to him, Ross wrapped his free arm around Lorna's waist. "I don't think you'd last long, lass. You were enjoying them earlier. You'd soon be going through withdrawals."

Lorna rolled her eyes. "I half expected you to say they were the greatest gifts of my lifetime."

He grinned. "I did think about it." He winked and Lorna chuckled. "But the bigger question is whether you're okay with me claiming you to the clan by holding your hand, especially before talking with your children. Fraser, in particular, might not be happy about it."

She sighed. "He's protective, like his late father. But leave Fraser to me. I was hoping we could talk to all of the children at dinner tonight. On the off chance we see them on the way home, I'll handle it. Holding hands isn't exactly a mate vow."

"Well, for dinner, just make sure to hide the breakables."

Hitting his chest, Lorna scowled. "There won't be any throwing. I'm going to make that very clear at the beginning of our discussion."

"Right, because the MacKenzies always sit prim and proper at the dinner table."

"If anything happens, then stand your own. Otherwise, you won't survive being part of the family."

Ross's heart skipped a beat. "So, you want me to be part of your family, Lorna?"

Searching his eyes, she finally murmured, "Perhaps, Ross. But you're going to have to earn the place. Not just with me or my dragon, but my children as well."

Lightly caressing her cheek, he answered, "Oh, I will. I think I'm already halfway there."

Lorna frowned but then smiled. "I would deny it, but I'm too old to lie. I've grown used to having you around, human, so I hope you can win over more hearts than mine."

He tried not to pin too much hope on Lorna's mention of winning hearts. He was falling in love with her already. But Ross wasn't going to rush things.

Best to distract both himself and Lorna with touch. "Oh, I'm quite the charmer, especially when I'm determined." He kissed her jaw. "And believe me, Lorna, I'm determined to have all of you." He nipped her bottom lip. "It should be a breeze."

Lorna snorted, but he cut off her reply with a kiss. As the beautiful dragonwoman in his arms melted against him, Ross only hoped his cockiness would prove to be true. Now that he'd kissed her, he wanted a future with Lorna MacKenzie, no matter what it took.

The Dragon's Heart

~~~

Lorna somehow managed to stand tall and avoid barking at the clan members staring as she and Ross walked hand in hand. It helped that every few seconds Ross squeezed her fingers in reassurance.

She rather liked his warm, strong hands.

Her dragon spoke up. *Just wait until they touch other parts of our body. I think Ross's wicked sense of humor will translate into a different type of wicked in bed.*

Hush. You're acting as if we're twenty and in the throes of early dragon lust.

Her beast huffed. *Well, it's close. I have more than twenty years to make up for.*

Lorna was trying to think of how to reply to that when the curvy, gray-haired figure of Meg Boyd stepped into her path.

Meg and Lorna were the same age and had been friends-slash-rivals their entire lives. Each pushed the other to be a bit better, but sometimes, Lorna could do with a break.

The present was one of those times. She didn't need Meg badgering Ross or trying to win him over. If Meg did try, then Lorna would have to give the female a tongue-lashing. Now that Lorna had given in to Ross's kisses, she wanted to keep him.

Possessiveness didn't fade with age when it came to dragon-shifters.

Lorna's dragon huffed. *It's not our fault Ross picked us over Meg. Maybe if you introduce Meg to Stu, she'll focus her attentions elsewhere. Then we all win.*

There's an idea. Clever beast.

I do have my uses from time to time.

To keep from laughing, Lorna cleared her throat. Meeting Meg's eyes, Lorna asked, "Can we help you with something, Meg?"

Meg looked from Lorna to Ross and back again, her gaze lingering an extra second on their clasped hands. "Aye, you can start by telling me how long this has been going on."

"If you were as good a gossip as you claim to be, then you should know the answer to that," Lorna replied. Damn, why was she goading the female?

Meg shook her head. "There's no need to be rude, Lorna. I may have fancied Ross in the beginning, but ol' Archie has been courting me these past few weeks. If you'd ever come over to visit, you would know that by now."

Lorna blinked. Archie MacAllister was notorious for his long-time feud with his neighbor Cal, which often sent one or both of them to the surgery. "I sure hope you're avoiding his place. It's not exactly safe there, aye?"

Meg waved a hand. "Cal would never hurt me. I've been working my charms on him as well."

"Wait a second. You have two males after you?" Lorna asked.

Meg frowned. "You don't have to sound so surprised. Females are rarer, after all, and even more so at our age. Once I gave one male a chance, I couldn't resist the other."

"That isn't going to end well, Meg," Lorna pointed out. "Dragon males don't share. Most especially that pair. I've lost count of the number of sheep they've stolen from each other, let alone how many boulders they've dropped onto each other's property. I'm surprised their cottages are still standing."

Meg sniffed. "Everything will turn out fine. I know what I'm doing." She leaned forward. "Come over soon and we can compare notes."

From the corner of Lorna's eye, she saw Ross's jaw drop. She murmured, "What's the matter, Ross? You afraid the dragon males will outdo you?"

"Of course not," he barked. "But I'd rather not air my private life to all the world."

Lorna grinned. "It's a bit late for that."

Before Ross could answer, Faye—Lorna's only daughter— asked from behind, "Mum? When did you officially get together with Ross?"

Everyone turned to face the tall dragonwoman with wild, curly hair and the same whiskey eyes as Lorna.

Ross spoke up before Lorna could. "I'm surprised you're asking, Faye, my dear. You're the one always teasing about us getting together."

Faye's gaze moved to Lorna. "Does Fraser know?"

"Not yet," Lorna answered. "Although I'm bringing it up at dinner."

Faye's eyes lit up with excitement. "Can I be the one to tell him? Please, Mum?"

"I'm not sure that's the best idea, hen. Fraser will require a delicacy you don't possess," Lorna stated.

"Nonsense. It's every younger sister's duty to irritate her older brother. I'm not sure I'll be able to top this anytime soon. I don't think Holly will name their bairn Faye after me, so I really need this," Faye answered.

Ross chuckled at her side. "It might be best, Lorna. That way Fraser can take out his frustrations on Faye. Once she wears him down with a challenge or two, then I can talk with the lad."

Lorna raised an eyebrow. "By talk, you mean argue."

He shrugged. "Maybe, maybe not. With Fergus and Holly there, they might be able to talk some sense into him. They each have a way of calming the lad down."

Faye laid a hand on Lorna's forearm. "Mum, let me share the news and I'll clean the bathroom for a month."

"You're supposed to be cleaning it anyway," Lorna pointed out.

"Details, details. So, what's the verdict?" Faye leaned forward as she asked.

Lorna met Ross's gaze and he shrugged. "I say yes."

Lorna sighed. "Already you're going to spoil the youngest."

He winked. "Aye, but of course. What's a stepfather to do but spoil? I'm going to need Faye on my side."

Faye all but bounced in place. "I think I'm going to like having Ross around."

Shaking her head, Lorna finally answered, "Fine. But at the first sign of a challenge or fight, you take it outside. Understand?"

"Yes, Mum." Faye kissed her cheek and then clapped Ross's shoulder. "Tonight is going be bloody brilliant."

Before Lorna or Ross could get another word in, Faye rushed off to do who knew what.

Releasing Lorna's hand, Ross wrapped an arm around her waist. "You'd better cook a fabulous dinner tonight, love. Only food might distract everyone enough to keep from killing each other."

Lorna shook her head. "And who's fault is that? I don't know why I let you talk me into Faye's request."

"Come, Lorna. You can worry about the bairns later. We have a dinner to make." He leaned down to her ear and whispered, "And I want a few more kisses along the way."

Meg, still standing nearby, giggled. "I always knew Ross would be insatiable." She stood taller. "Not that he can compare to my Archie and Cal."

"Of course not," Lorna murmured to humor her friend.

Meg shooed them off. "Go get ready for your dinner. I'll stop by tomorrow to hear what happened."

Before Lorna could protest, Meg was halfway across the clearing. Ross's whisper filled her ear. "Half the clan will hear about us before night falls. I think a batch of your famous scones are in order to placate the children."

With a sigh, Lorna leaned against Ross. "I'm tempted to put sleeping drugs into them and put this off until tomorrow."

"Don't be a coward, Lorna. I've never known you to be one, so don't start now."

Her dragon chimed in. *He's right.*

It didn't take you long to start siding with Ross.

It's been a long time since I could side with someone against you. I could never win if I tried with our children. Ross, on the other hand, I think can win occasionally.

After decades of doing things her way, Lorna expected to feel angry or irritated with her beast. Instead, she wanted to sigh in relief at not having to be in charge twenty-four seven for her entire brood. Just picturing Ross standing guard over her food while she cooked and shooing away Faye and Fraser made her smile.

Lorna would never truly give up her power or strength, but she would like to hand over the little things to someone else. Maybe then her remaining blonde hairs would stay blonde a wee bit longer.

She finally answered, "I won't put it off, of course. But we'd better hurry, or I won't have time to cook, let alone kiss you."

49

"So you are thinking of my kisses, aye?"

"More like you're thinking of mine."

Ross chuckled. "That I am, love. That I am."

Smiling, Lorna motioned with her head. "Now that you've admitted one of your weaknesses, we can go."

As they walked, Ross answered, "So if I keep mentioning how much I'm thinking of your kisses, you'll give me what I want?"

"I didn't say that." Ross gave a mock look of hurt and Lorna snorted. "I thought you were too old for games."

"Now, now, we need a few games or life might grow dull. And believe me, Lorna, I have many, many games I want to play with you."

Ross's words held a double meaning. Combined with the heat in his eyes, Lorna barely resisted a shiver.

Her dragon spoke up. *Little does he know, I have games for him, too.*

Oh, dear. Between her dragon and her frisky human, Lorna was going to be in for an interesting night.

And she was rather looking forward to it.

CHAPTER FIVE

Ross watched as Lorna bent over to check the roast in the oven. He'd always had to watch Lorna cook on the sly before, but now, he simply admired her arse.

Lorna's voice boomed out. "I feel your eyes on my bum, Ross. Have you finished chopping the veg for the salad?"

Picking up the knife on the counter, Ross focused back on the cucumber on the chopping board. "I was just reaching for the next one."

"Liar," she said as she closed the oven door and turned toward him. But rather than irritation, amusement danced in Lorna's eyes.

Ross grinned. "I think you like my eyes on your arse."

"If you want me to answer that, then you'd better start chopping."

"So you do, then, lass."

"I'm far too old to be a lass."

"Says who?"

Faye's voice drifted into the room. "Says me. Please stop flirting with my mum until later. It's bad enough I caught you snogging her half an hour ago."

Ross raised his brows. "That's what you get for not knocking, my dear. Enter at your own risk next time."

"Ross," Lorna scolded at the same time Faye answered, "I really should find my own place. I'll never be able to unsee that."

Faye made a beeline for the chopped tomatoes, but Ross moved the plate away. "If we start charging you for food by the pound, then you might think about finding your own place even sooner."

Reaching for a scone, Faye frowned. "Mum wouldn't do that."

Lorna whisked the plate away before Faye could touch it. "I just might. I could probably travel the world with the money I saved." Lorna placed a hand on her hip. "But we can discuss this later. Are your brothers nearly here?"

Faye shrugged. "Probably. They don't report their every move to me."

Lorna sighed, but Ross spoke up first. "Aye, well, that just means you can set the table yourself."

"Me? But I'm rubbish at folding napkins."

"As long as they're clean and reasonably close to a plate, that will be fine," Ross stated.

Faye stared at Ross but finally moved toward one of the cupboards. "I know you just want to be alone with my mum. I'd protest, but it increases the chance of Fraser finding you. And I'm looking forward to that."

Lorna jumped in. "Faye Cleopatra MacKenzie, set the table and leave us in peace, or I really will start charging you by the pound for your food."

Muttering something Ross couldn't hear, Faye took a stack of plates and exited into the dining room.

Ross put down his knife and moved to Lorna's side. After kissing her cheek, he murmured, "You'll miss her more when she's gone."

"I know. Normally, I can handle Faye, but I'm just nervous about tonight."

"Don't worry, Lorna. Fraser may be protective, but once he sees me taking care of you, he'll open up."

Lorna tilted her head. "Aye, well, Fergus just arrived. So you can warm up to him, first. Don't let his quieter nature fool you. He can be as fierce as either of his siblings."

"Even if it means challenging both of your lads to a wrestling match to prove my worth, I'll do it." He caressed her cheek. "You're worth it, Lorna MacKenzie."

Lorna's expression softened. He wanted to say it was affection, but Ross didn't want to hope too soon for anything. Even though they'd spent many months together, winning Lorna's heart was an entirely different thing, no matter how much the dragonwoman had already won over his.

He murmured, "Let's see how he reacts, then."

Just as the kitchen door opened, Ross kissed Lorna.

~~~

If Lorna were completely rational, she'd push Ross away and greet Fergus. But as her human slid his tongue between her lips and gently caressed her lower back, she could barely string two thoughts together.

Between Ross acting like a parent to Faye and then kissing Lorna as if she were the most beautiful female in the world, she was starting to get her hopes up for the future.

It was Gina's voice—Fergus's American human mate—that finally caused Lorna to pull away from Ross. "See, Fergus. I knew they would hookup."

Before Fergus could reply, Gina's younger sister, Kaylee, clapped her hands and jumped in. "I just won my bet with Fraser! He will have to take me up into the air in his dragon form now."

Gina adjusted the sleeping bairn in her arms and scowled at Kaylee. "It had better be in a basket."

Kaylee shrugged. "Maybe, maybe not. I didn't specify."

As the American females argued, Lorna studied Fergus's expression, but couldn't detect any emotion in his eyes. So, she asked her oldest son, "What are you thinking, Fergus?"

Gina and Kaylee quieted down to stare at Fergus. He finally replied, "As long as he makes you happy, that's good enough for me." Fergus's pupils flashed to slits and back as he moved his gaze to Ross. "But hurt my mum and I don't care if you're Holly's father, I will personally carry you back to Aberdeen as many times as it takes to keep you away from her."

Ross nodded. "Aye, I'd expect nothing less."

Fergus nodded back. "Good. But you're on your own with Fraser."

Gina adjusted the blanket around wee Jamie. "Fraser will come around. Considering what happened with you and Holly last year, he should understand that love crops up in unusual places."

Holly had originally been a sacrifice and assigned to Fergus. However, Holly had ended up being Fraser's true mate, and it'd taken quite a bit to clean up the resulting mess with the Department of Dragon Affairs.

Lorna ignored the word "love," but didn't dismiss it. Her feelings were too jumbled to make much sense of them.

Her dragon snorted. *I know what they are.*

Ignoring her beast, Lorna moved to her grandbaby. Caressing Jamie's cheek, she murmured, "If wee Jamie stays asleep, Fraser will at least keep his voice down."

Fergus drawled, "Glad to see you're going to use my son as a buffer."

Lorna frowned but kept her tone light for the bairn. "Jamie doesn't mind. After all, he's grandma's wee lad."

Gina offered Jamie, but Lorna shook her head. "Until I can teach you to cook a proper roast, I'm stuck in the kitchen."

Kaylee spoke up. "I'm the better cook out of the two of us. Can I watch? Maybe next time, I can even do it all by myself and finally be able to do more than waitress at the clan's main restaurant."

"It's going to take more than one lesson, hen," Lorna answered. "But I'm not one to turn down an offer of help." She looked to Ross. "Then maybe Ross can finish chopping more than two tomatoes."

Ross sighed dramatically. "And there you go belittling my achievements for the day."

Faye entered the kitchen again. "I think you've had a few more than that." She grinned at Lorna and looked back to Ross. "Or, at least my mother would agree."

"Faye," Lorna scolded.

Faye put her palms up and shrugged. "If you were expecting us not to tease you, then you don't know us at all."

"Scamp," Lorna answered with a smile. "Finish setting the table. Fergus just volunteered to help you." Fergus grunted, but Lorna continued before he could say anything. "And Gina can watch to make sure you two finish without dallying."

Fergus looked to Gina and the young female grinned. "I can manage that. I know how Fergus likes to be ordered around."

Leaning down to Gina's ear, Fergus murmured, "You're going to pay for that later."

The American laughed, and Lorna looked to Ross. As they shared their own smile, Lorna hoped she'd one day have what her sons had with their mates.

After all this time, Lorna was beginning to think she had room for two men in her heart.

Her dragon hummed, which snapped Lorna back to the present. Shooing her children to go set the table, she guided Kaylee into the kitchen. As she went over her recipe and instructions for her infamous roast, Lorna resisted looking to Ross; otherwise, she'd never be able to concentrate.

Yes, Lorna Stewart MacKenzie was acting like an infatuated lass of twenty. But for once, she didn't care.

~~~

As Ross reached for another cucumber, it took everything he had not to turn around and stare at Lorna again.

She might hide it well, but she was pleased with Fergus and Faye's acceptance. That only left Fraser to win over before Lorna would stop fretting and allow him to claim her completely.

However, Fraser was going to be tricky, especially since Holly was pregnant and none of them wanted to upset her. His daughter had lost a bairn last year because of a miscarriage, and he didn't want to do anything to cause her stress.

Yet showing weakness with Fraser would most assuredly not end well. The dragonman liked to get his way, and Ross wasn't about to give in.

Faye rushed into the kitchen, interrupting his thoughts. Anticipation danced in her eyes as she blurted out, "Fraser's here."

THE DRAGON'S HEART

Ross had long ago ceased asking how the dragon-shifters knew someone had arrived; he'd just receive another lecture about their bloody brilliant hearing.

He'd be lying if he wasn't a bit jealous. But there wasn't a magic potion that turned a human into a dragon-shifter, so Ross had learned to accept his shortcomings with the dragons of Lochguard. Besides, humans had their charms. No doubt Lorna's dragon would love all of Ross's attention since he didn't have his own dragon to worry about.

Wiping his hands on a tea towel, Ross turned toward the other kitchen entrance just as Holly entered with Fraser right behind her.

Ross opened his arms, and Holly gave him a hug. He asked, "How's my bonny lass today?"

"Fine, Dad. I spent most of the day helping Dr. Innes and Layla with painting the surgery."

The surgery was one of the buildings that had nearly been destroyed in the attack a few months earlier. "Good. With Innes there, he'll make sure you don't lift anything you shouldn't."

Holly sighed as Fraser nodded. The dragonman's eyes were full of approval. "Exactly. Innes is keeping a close eye on her."

Holly frowned up at Fraser. "I'm a midwife, Fraser. I know the limitations of a pregnant woman."

"Not when it comes to yourself, love," Fraser answered. "I won't ask you to give up your job, but I just want you to be careful. Carrying twins is twice as hard."

Ross blinked. "Twins? When did you find this out?"

Holly grinned at her dad. "Today at my first ultrasound."

Ross engulfed Holly in a hug. "Congrats, Holly-berry. That gives me twice the grandkids to spoil."

"Dad," Holly scolded halfheartedly as she hugged him tightly.

Lorna's voice came from beside him. "Stopping hogging Holly. Let me have a turn, Ross."

"Sorry, love," Ross answered as he released his daughter and let Lorna have a turn.

"Love?" Fraser echoed.

Bloody hell. He'd never used "love" with Lorna before today. Leave it to him to ruin what should be a happy moment for his daughter. "Aye, love. I care for your mother."

Narrowing his eyes, Fraser took a step toward Ross. "I thought I told you to stay away from my mum."

Lorna jumped in. "Fraser MacKenzie."

Ross put up a hand. "I will deal with him."

Lorna sighed. "Males. I give up. Come, Holly, let's tell Gina the news."

Ross was vaguely aware of Lorna and the others leaving, but he refused to break his gaze with Fraser. If he didn't take care of Lorna's protective son now, it would cause more stress for all, including Holly.

Once they were alone, Fraser spoke again. "I'm not sure you're worthy enough for my mother."

Raising an eyebrow, Ross asked, "And why not?"

"Because you're not my father."

"Look, lad. I'm not trying to replace your father. But it's been nearly thirty years and your mum is lonely. Would you deny her happiness in her later years?"

"She is happy, human. You just like to take advantage of free cooking and board."

With a growl, Ross closed the distance between. "Your mum deserves more respect than that, Fraser. She is one of the most independent women I know, and there's no bloody way she'd tolerate someone taking advantage of her. Are you saying different?"

"Of course not," Fraser muttered.

"Then what?" When Fraser remained silent, Ross remembered something Gina had said earlier. "You of all men should know that love and attraction aren't planned."

"This isn't the same. I doubt you're my mum's true mate."

"Aye, you're right. I'm not. But that doesn't keep me from thinking she's the most beautiful woman on Lochguard. Hell, maybe even in Scotland."

Fraser studied him for a few seconds before replying, "And how do I know you're not spouting fancy words? My mum's been hurt before when my dad died, and it devastated her. I might've been young, but I remember enough. I don't ever want her to go through that again."

"I don't want to hurt your mother. I've had months and months to get to know her. We suit. Not only that, she's a great kisser."

Fraser frowned. "I don't want to think of you kissing my mum."

"Scowl all you like, lad. One day you'll be my age and understand. Unless you're suddenly going to stop wanting to kiss my daughter when she hits her sixties."

"Of course not. Holly is my true mate, and I love her. I'll always want her."

"Aye, well, just because I'm not your mum's true mate doesn't mean I don't want her with every bit of my being. All I ask is for you to allow your mother to fight her own battles. If she becomes fed up, we both know she'll toss me out on my arse. If she feels quite the opposite, then you should want your mother to be happy and feel loved."

When Fraser didn't answer straight way, Ross merely waited. This was the first real conversation he'd had with his son-in-law since meeting him. Truth and candor seemed to be working with the lad better than Ross had hoped.

Fraser finally spoke up again. "I will give you a chance, but don't think I won't be watching you."

Ross put out a hand, and Fraser took it. After shaking, he answered, "That I can live with. Now, how about we celebrate your own twins and leave the arguing here in the kitchen? For Holly, if nothing else."

At the mention of the twins, Fraser smiled and stood a little taller. "Aye, let's celebrate."

As Ross and his son-in-law exited the kitchen, Ross met Lorna's gaze. With a nod, he moved to Lorna's side and wrapped an arm around her.

Fraser was busy talking to Holly's abdomen about adventures while Fergus merely shook his head. Faye was snacking on a pilfered scone next to Gina and Kaylee.

A sense of contentment settled over Ross. Between his daughter, his new family, and Lorna at his side, everything looked to be going well. For so long, Ross and Holly had been on their own. It was a nice change to have a dining room full of people.

Just as Lorna laid her head on Ross's shoulder, Finlay Stewart, the leader of Clan Lochguard and Lorna's nephew, entered the room with his heavily pregnant mate, Arabella. Everyone quieted down at Finn's presence.

Finn's gaze narrowed in on Ross and Lorna. Then he sighed. "Why does my family keep making my job so bloody difficult?"

CHAPTER SIX

Lorna clicked her tongue at her nephew. "No one ever said being clan leader would be easy. It's good to test your limits once in a while."

Fraser chimed in. "Lorna and Ross getting together is old news. Guess what, cousin? You're going to have twin nieces or nephews to play with your triplets. I know technically they're you're cousins, but we're calling you uncle. That way, you can spoil them more."

Arabella blinked. "Holly is having twins?"

Holly smiled. "Yes, we found out earlier today. The replacement ultrasound equipment finally came in, and I was the first patient."

Finn put up an arm to stop Arabella from moving. "Hold on a second. Talking about Fraser's twins can wait." He waved toward Lorna and Ross. "When did this happen?"

Arabella shook her head and pushed Finn's arm away. "It's been happening for a while, Finn. You need to pay better attention."

"But, Ara, I want to focus all of my attention on you."

"I hit my third trimester last week, and I feel so much better. You should spend more time on the clan before the babies come," she answered as she moved to Holly's side.

Finn sighed again. "And here I was trying to be the devoted mate."

Lorna jumped in. "Stop with the theatrics, Finlay. Ara says she's feeling better, so there's no need to hover. She'll ask for help if she needs it. Isn't that right, child?"

Arabella nodded. "I learned my lesson the hard way."

Lorna looked back to Finn. "Right, that's settled. So what's your concern about Ross and me? He already has permission to stay on Lochguard indefinitely. There's little else for you to do, except maybe get me a larger dining room table. With all the grand babies, we're going to need the space."

"What about if you wish to mate him, Aunt Lorna? Then what?" Finn asked.

Lorna's dragon hummed at the word "mate," but Lorna ignored her beast. "We'll deal with that as it comes. Considering that Nikki lass mated her human, I imagine the new director of the Department of Dragon Affairs will want to have other special ceremonies. What better PR than having an older couple?"

Ross cleared his throat. "Do I get a say in this, love?"

"In real life, aye. In hypotheticals, no. I'm trying to make a point to Finlay," Lorna answered.

Her human chuckled. "It doesn't have to be a contest, love. Why don't we talk about all this later, if and when it becomes relevant? We both just found out we're going to have two new grandkids coming. I think we should celebrate that."

Lorna's dragon spoke up. *He's right. We haven't even claimed him yet. Let's do that first and then Ross will convince Finn to help us.*

You're moving a wee bit fast for my liking, dragon.

I know what I want, and that's good enough for me. Hesitating is for the young.

I would argue, but I want to celebrate Fraser and Holly's news.

Pushing her beast to the back of her mind, Lorna looked back to her nephew. "We'll revisit the situation later, Finlay."

Finn grinned as he moved to Ross's side and gripped his shoulder. "I think I'm going to like having Ross around."

Lorna rolled her eyes. "You just say that because you can weasel your way out of answering questions."

Finn looked affronted. "And here I was trying to be supportive of my aunt."

Arabella's voice cut in. "Finn, leave it alone. You need to convince your cousin not to corrupt his children. You know the newest MacKenzie twins will corrupt our own babies, and I definitely don't need three mini-Finns or Frasers running around."

"But we're the most lovable, Ara. Not to mention entertaining," Finn answered with a wink.

Fergus grunted. "I say it's more like a string of never-ending headaches. Don't worry, Ara. I'll help keep your triplets as uncorrupted as possible. I'm sure wee Jamie will help keep them all in line, too."

Fraser rubbed his hands together. "You just made it a challenge, brother. And I'm out to win." He gestured to the sleeping baby in Gina's arms. "That includes corrupting Mac-squared."

"Don't call my son that ridiculous nickname," Fergus growled.

Fraser shrugged. "Hey, you and Gina gave him the surname of MacDonald-MacKenzie. It's your own fault."

As Fraser and Fergus continued to argue, Ross whispered into Lorna's ear, "How much longer until dinner's ready?"

"Really? You're thinking with your stomach right now?"

His voice dropped an octave, which made her shiver. "No, Lorna. The sooner you feed everyone, the sooner you can kick them out. I want you all to myself."

"Oh," Lorna said as her cheeks flushed with heat.

"You'd better work on that flush of yours. While I love seeing the color on your cheeks, your children will tease you."

Turning her head, Lorna met Ross's gaze. "You know what? Now that we've talked with them, and they know what's going on, I don't care. How about we give them a show?"

Ross wrapped his arms around her waist and murmured, "I like your way of thinking, woman."

Impatient, Lorna took Ross's lips in a kiss and pulled him close. Lorna was vaguely aware of whistles and comments, but she ignored them. Ross had passed the initial test with her children, and she was impatient for what came next.

Her dragon hummed. *Yes, yes. Kick them out now.*

Not yet.

She was going to say more, but Ross growled and heat spread throughout her body.

Her beast spoke up again. *Send everyone away. I want him.*

Lorna agreed with her dragon. Lorna was going to serve dinner as quickly as possible and send everyone packing. It was time to claim her new male.

~~~

Nearly two hours later, Ross placed the last bit of leftovers into the fridge and shut the door with a flourish.

He turned around to see Lorna leaning against the counter, watching him. Her pupils flashed to slits and back. He grinned. "Is your dragon burning for ol' Ross Anderson?"

She raised her brows. "Wouldn't you like to know."

Closing the distance between them, Ross pulled Lorna up against him. The softness of her body made him hard. With Lorna, he wouldn't need any pills to do the deed.

He nipped her earlobe and whispered, "I know one way to get the information out of you." He worried her flesh again before adding, "Of course, it involves you naked on a bed."

"Ross," Lorna said in a breathy whisper.

"Don't tell me you're shy about this, love. Because I'm not."

Lorna pulled back to meet his gaze. The heat he saw there eased some of his worry.

The dragonwoman tilted her head. "Not shy, exactly. But it's been awhile. I may need you to remind me of a few things."

He snorted. "I think you just want me to do all the work."

She ran her hand up his chest to behind his neck. The soft strum of her fingers sent a spark down his back and straight to his groin.

If that wasn't enough, Lorna leaned forward until her soft breasts squashed against his chest. The hard points of her nipples were too much, and he let out a small groan.

Smiling, Lorna replied, "Not all the work, but I did just cook a huge meal and all you did was chop veg. I think you have more energy than me."

"So is that the tradeoff? You cook, and I give you fantastic sex?"

"You wouldn't hear any complaints from me."

Ross chuckled. "Aye, well, I'd better start paying off my debt."

Before Lorna could reply, he took her lips in a possessive kiss. As he explored the inside of her mouth, he ran a hand under her jumper to her warm skin. He stroked circles slowly against her back until Lorna sighed.

Breaking the kiss, Ross murmured, "We can save the kitchen counter for later. Right now, I want to see you naked on our bed."

"So my bed is now our bed?"

"Yes." He nipped her bottom lip. "I can't have any other dragonmen getting ideas about moving in and stealing you away."

Lorna paused, and Ross wondered if he'd pushed too fast. But considering he and Lorna had lived in close proximity for months, he wasn't exactly a stranger.

Still, the thought of another man not her late mate in that bed might be too much. Maybe he was daft for suggesting her bed instead of his.

Then Lorna kissed his jaw. "No one is going to sneak in, you fool. If they tried, I have a homemade deterrent to keep them away."

"Oh, aye? Should I be worried?"

"Not as long as you stay on my good side, human."

"I'll keep that in mind." He kissed her nose. "Now, if I were twenty years younger, I'd sweep you off your feet and carry you up the stairs. But I don't want to break that old hip you keep mentioning."

Lorna chuckled. "Considering I'm not as light as I once was, we'd better be safe and walk."

"I don't care about what you looked like when you were younger. You're perfect to me now." He cupped her cheeks and stroked them with his thumbs. "Shall we go upstairs so I can devour you?"

Her pupils flashed before she smiled. "We'd better, or you might start dozing off."

He lightly smacked her bum. "Cheeky dragonwoman."

Lorna laughed, and the sound echoed inside the kitchen. Ross decided right then and there, he would be the one to make Lorna laugh for the rest of her days.

Releasing her, Ross took her hand and tugged. "Then let's get going before I fall asleep and snore your ear off."

They exited the kitchen and ascended the stairs. "You do snore loudly, unfortunately for me."

"That just means I'll have to lay on my side and hold you close, all through the night. I don't snore on my side."

Tenderness flashed in Lorna's eyes, and Ross ached to simply hold his dragonwoman in his arms.

But he was fairly certain his hard cock and Lorna's flashing dragon eyes weren't going to let that happen.

As soon as they entered Lorna's room, she shut the door and released his hand. Ross was about to ask what she was doing when Lorna tugged off her jumper, and all thoughts left his head.

~~~

With her heart thumping inside her chest, Lorna somehow managed to swiftly tug off her jumper and toss it aside as if she did it every day. Maybe she could fool Ross into thinking she was confident about taking him to bed. After all, it had been decades. The last time had been with Jamie.

Jamie. For a split second, Lorna wondered if she were being selfish in wanting Ross. She and Jamie had always promised to look out for the children if one of them were gone. Lorna's children still needed her help with the babies and new mates. Faye, in particular, was still healing from her wing injury the year before.

Her dragon growled. *Why is this so difficult? All of the bairns are adults. They need space to grow and strengthen their new families.*

My mother helped me when I was a new mum. I should do the same.

Aye, and you will. But what about the mornings or nights? Soon we'll be all alone in this house.

Ross's voice interrupted her conversation. "What's the matter, Lorna? Are you having second thoughts?"

Her beast growled. *Look at the desire and heat in Ross's eyes. He wants us, and I want him. Don't you?*

Remembering Ross's kisses, his teasing, and even his companionship since arriving on Lochguard, Lorna knew she did.

Maybe it was time for Lorna to take some time for herself after raising four stubborn-headed children on her own.

Pushing aside her nervousness and doubts, Lorna answered, "Of course not. A little waiting might do you good."

Chuckling, Ross winked. "Not too long, I hope. It's getting close to my bedtime."

Lorna shook her head and moved her hands to her skirt. After wiggling out of it, she yanked off her socks and stopped at the hem of her panties. Once they were off, she doubted she would be able to stop her dragon from claiming Ross.

Ross's voice was husky as he said, "Show me, love. I want to see all of you."

The wanting in his voice gave Lorna the courage she needed to slide off her panties and undo her bra. Even though the room was warm, she shivered. Ross's long perusal of her body only made her heart pound harder and wetness pool between her legs.

In the next second, Ross tugged off his shirt and her eyes moved to the gray hair on his chest. While Ross wasn't a dragon-shifter, he had a lean hardness to him that she looked forward to touching and exploring with both her hands and her tongue.

"Like what you see, love?"

Frowning, Lorna motioned toward his trousers. "Hurry up and take them off before I freeze to death."

With a chuckle, Ross unzipped his trousers and dropped them to the floor. His erection punched against his underwear and her dragon growled in impatience. *Tell him to hurry up. I'm starving.*

Before she could think of how to reply to that, Ross pulled down his underwear and stood tall. Unable to resist, she looked down his lean, tall body until she reached his long, hard cock.

His desire for her was plain to see.

Of course it is. You need more confidence when it comes to our attractiveness.

Shut it, dragon.

Ross strode up to her and pulled her against his warm body. The press of his erection against her belly caused a pounding ache between her thighs.

After a brief kiss, Ross guided them back toward the bed. "I hope you're ready, Lorna." He gently guided her down to the mattress and caged her body with his arms. "Because I'm not stopping until you scream my name at least twice."

She was about to say that was a tall order, but Ross's fingers brushed the juncture between her legs and she sucked in a breath.

Chapter Seven

Only because of his formidable self-control, could Ross caress Lorna's most sensitive flesh and take his time. With each stroke of his fingers, Lorna's legs parted a little more. The flush of her cheeks was a lovely contrast to her blondish gray hair fanned out behind her head.

Damn, she was gorgeous.

It'd been a long time since he'd last made love to a woman and regardless of what his brain wanted, his cock wanted to thrust into his dragonwoman and claim her straightaway.

Lorna's breathy voice caught his attention. "Ross, please."

Hearing his name on her lips was the tipping point. Removing his hand, Ross positioned his cock at her entrance. "Ready, love?"

With her pupils flashing, she murmured, "Hurry up."

Not wanting to keep his woman waiting any longer, Ross inched his way inside. Lorna might not be a virgin, but it had been a while, and he didn't want to hurt her.

As if reading his mind, Lorna growled, "Don't you dare be delicate with me, Ross. I want the fire and passion I know is there."

Lowering his head, Ross nipped Lorna's bottom lip. "As you wish."

THE DRAGON'S HEART

Thrusting the rest of the way inside, Lorna moaned and grabbed his biceps. She dug in her nails, and something primal sparked inside Ross.

He moved his hips and increased his pace with each movement. He loved the way Lorna gripped his cock with just the right amount of pressure.

However, he wanted to feel more than just his cock inside his dragonwoman. Transferring his weight to his left arm, Ross cupped Lorna's breast and squeezed. The large, warm flesh was softer than he'd imagined.

But touching wasn't enough. He pinched her hard nipple between his fingers and Lorna moaned. "Yes."

Sucking her nipples and worrying them with his teeth would have to wait. Ross needed to make Lorna his. The desire to hear her scream as she came only pushed his hips faster.

Yet as the pressure built at the base of his spine, Ross gritted his teeth. He wouldn't come like a lad of fifteen before Lorna. His dragonwoman deserved better.

He glided his hand down Lorna's soft stomach to the hair at the juncture of her thighs. Finding her hard nub, Ross rubbed it in firm circles. Lorna squirmed her hips below him. When she dug her nails further into his skin, Ross wanted to let go.

Thankfully, Lorna screamed his name and arched her back. As she gripped and released his cock, Ross roared and stilled inside her. Pleasure raced and crashed through his body as he finally made Lorna MacKenzie his own.

Once she had wrung every last drop out of him, Ross collapsed on top of her.

For a short while, they both merely lay there, breathing heavily. Then Lorna's nails lightly traced his back as she purred, "You still have a few tricks left in you, old man."

With a grunt, Ross rolled to the side and took Lorna with him. The dragonwoman laid half on his chest, which gave him the perfect opportunity to grab her arse cheek and squeeze. "I'm more interested in seeing your tricks, love."

Lorna raised her head. "I thought we had a deal? I cook and you give me fantastic sex."

"So you think it's fantastic, aye? Good to know. Maybe it'll make all the dragonmen jealous."

"Don't you dare go bragging to the public, Ross Anderson. What happens in this bed is private."

Ross swept Lorna's long hair over her shoulder and then traced her collarbone. "So does that give me leave to do whatever I wish as long as I don't go havering on about it?"

Leaning down, Lorna whispered into his ear, "I can't answer that question yet. I need to see more of your moves to make a better-informed decision."

He chuckled. "You just want me to do all of the work."

Lorna moved to straddle his hips, her lovely curves in full view. Not waiting for a reply, he traced her breast, her waist, and the stretch marks on her belly. Meeting Lorna's gaze, he noticed her expression had shuttered. She was hiding something. "Tell me what's on your mind, love."

~~~

Lorna was raring to go another round with her human. The things that man could do with his fingers made her skin burn.

Then he studied her body and lingered on her belly, and Lorna's confidence faded. Between wrinkles and stretch marks, she wondered how Ross found her beautiful at all.

THE DRAGON'S HEART

Her dragon huffed. *Remember our talk before, about self-confidence? We're gorgeous. Accept it.*

As she tried to think of how to reply, Ross's voice interrupted her thoughts. "Tell me what's on your mind, love."

Looking down at her human, Lorna saw concern in his gaze. Her dragon chimed in again. *You're being foolish, and I don't like it.*

Ross stroked her back in slow circles, and she sighed. "I just wish I'd met you years ago."

He raised his brows. "But would you have been ready then? I somehow doubt it. Every heart needs time to heal, some more than others. I never thought I'd be able to accept Anne was gone and to find someone else, but I did. Hell, I'm even glad of the cancer now, since it brought me to you and my second chance."

Placing her hands on his chest, Lorna teased his chest hair with her palms. "Those are fancy words considering we only kissed this morning."

Ross rolled them over until he caged her with his arms. "It's been nearly half a year since we met and I don't know about you, but I've treasured most of the days."

"Most?"

"Aye, the constant bickering with your youngest son I could've done without."

She smiled. "His protectiveness comes from his father. His spirit might have come from me."

"Might have?"

She chuckled. "Okay, all of it did come from me." She remained quiet a minute. When she finally replied, her voice was sober. "I still miss him, you know. Jamie."

Ross caressed her cheek. "Aye, I know. I miss my Anne every day. But I think she would've liked you. Even though Anne

73

was quiet, she was stubborn and strong-willed. She found creative ways to get her way."

"Jamie was a wee bit possessive, but deep down, I know he'd want me to be happy."

"Then why do you keep pushing the chance away, Lorna? One minute you can't get enough of me, and the next you shut down and keep me at arm's length. I don't like the latter, lass."

She searched Ross's eyes. This was one of those important moments in life when a person knew it could shape their future. If Lorna didn't open up to Ross now and speak the truth, she might lose her chance with him in the long run.

Her dragon spoke up. *Just tell him already so we can have more sex.*

Such a single-track mind.

We've done it your way for decades. Now, I want my way, too.

"So, is your dragon on my side?" Ross asked.

Lorna snorted. "Of course she is. I think she does it to get back at me for all the years of celibacy."

You have that right, her beast stated.

Ross replied before Lorna could, "Then maybe she could convince you to tell me why you pulled away earlier."

As Ross stroked her cheek, Lorna decided she was done with hesitating. She wanted Ross to know all of her. "It's been more than two decades since I've been with a male and my body has changed. I'm still getting used to being naked around you."

"Oh, aye? Then maybe I need to make you so used to my touch that it feels strange to be apart."

"Trying to charm me, human?"

He grinned. "Yes, and don't expect me to stop anytime soon."

Lorna laughed as Ross moved away to sit on his heels, his legs straddling the sides of her own.

He ran a finger across one shoulder and then the other. "These shoulders have had a lot to bear over the years, and yet they're still straight and strong." He moved his hand and laid his palm over her heart. "This heart is big enough to take in a nephew to raise, as well as an old man and even help with her daughter-in-law's sister."

Lorna should frown and tell him that almost anyone on Lochguard would do the same, but she didn't want to break the spell. Ross's husky words and gentle touch were addictive.

Ross cupped her breasts and gently lifted. "Not only did these nurture your bairns, but they also make any straight man dream of doing this." Leaning down, Ross took one of her nipples into his mouth and suckled. Each pull made her core pulse. Then he switched to the other one and Lorna bit her lip to keep from moaning.

Releasing her nipple with a flick of his tongue, Ross released her breasts to take hold of her wide hips. "And your hips. Hell, Lorna, they have just enough cushion to protect you from my fierce grip. And as for your arse,"—he slid one hand to under her arse cheek—"let's just say I can't wait to take you from behind. Your lovely arse will keep me from breaking my bones."

She smiled. "You're being silly. Sex isn't going to break you."

"I don't know." He thickened his accent. "I hear dragonwomen can be *verra* demanding in the bedroom."

Her dragon hummed. *He doesn't know the half of it. Just wait until I can wrest away control.*

Lorna opened her mouth to reply, but Ross placed a hand on her belly and rubbed slowly. If dragons could purr, Lorna would be doing it.

Her human said, "You display the scars of child-bearing, but more than that, they are a symbol of both the past and the future. Not having stretch marks or children wouldn't suit you, Lorna. You love to care for others, so embrace it."

Staring into Ross's eyes, Lorna saw truth. Her human truly believed everything he said about her.

Her beast huffed. *Between me and Ross, will you believe us now and embrace your sexiness?*

Ross took her hands and threaded his fingers through hers. "Have I convinced you of how much I want to see you naked yet, love? Because I can keep going."

Lorna blinked back tears and cleared her throat. "I'm glad you came into my life, Ross. You're a fine male and were more than worth waiting for."

He widened his eyes and gave a fake gasp. "Is Lorna MacKenzie actually opening up to me? Or am I dreaming?"

"Ross," she bit out.

Leaning down, Ross took her lips in a gentle kiss. "I've waited so many months for you, Lorna, that I'm ready to take you again." He brushed her cheek with his fingers. "Just don't expect this every night. An old man only has so much in him."

She smacked his bum. "Stop saying you're old. To me, you're just right." She nipped his bottom lip. "And let's see if we can get two more times out of you tonight."

"Someone's demanding."

"Aye, so get used to it."

Ross chuckled before taking her lips in a rough kiss. As his tongue slipped into her mouth, Lorna clutched his shoulder and pulled him close. With each stroke, Ross let her know how much he wanted her. And for the first time, Lorna didn't doubt herself or him.

CHAPTER EIGHT

Ross watched Lorna finish cooking up his breakfast in her nightshirt. He would've preferred her cooking in the nude, but given the proclivity of Lorna's children to show up unannounced, she'd convinced him of the necessity of wearing some clothing.

Yet he couldn't resist coming up behind her and taking her hips as he kissed her neck.

Despite leaning into his touch, she said, "Don't think your kisses are going to convince me to make you a full Scottish breakfast."

Stroking up and down her ribcage, Ross murmured, "You know how much I bloody hate porridge. Why are you making it yet again?"

"Because of your health. Not even your prowess in the bedroom will convince me to change my mind in this." She glanced at him. "I just found you, and I'm not about to lose you to a heart attack."

The fierceness in Lorna's gaze stole his breath away.

Kissing the side of her mouth, he replied, "My fierce dragon lass."

"Too right. Now step back or I may just drop a little of this down your pants."

He chuckled. "That's an empty threat, love, and you know it. Your dragon is quite fond of my 'prowess' as you put it."

"You're such a scamp."

"Aye, but you love that about me."

Lorna stared for a second more before turning back to her pan on the cooker. Ross's statement had been lighthearted, but he wondered if Lorna had taken it to mean more.

Ross had wanted the dragonwoman for so many months, he was practically in love with Lorna MacKenzie already. Not that he could tell her truthfully just yet. While cancer had put Ross's life and priorities in perspective, Lorna was still battling memories of her late husband. However, he hoped she didn't go back to keeping him at arm's length again. After the night before, Ross didn't think he could go back to being merely friends.

Blast, why was he even thinking about love and the future yet? It was too soon.

Ross barely resisted running a hand through his hair. Bloody hell, courting a woman was more difficult than he remembered.

Stepping back, Ross allowed Lorna to dish out their breakfast. When she finished, he took the bowls to the dining table and Lorna followed with the coffee and cutlery. They were just about to sit down when there was a knock on the door.

Lorna frowned. "My children rarely knock, so who stops by at eight in the morning that isn't family?"

She moved to answer the door, but Ross moved in front of her. "Let me. Your nightgown is too thin for strangers."

Amusement danced in her eyes. "I'd hardly call the people of Lochguard strangers."

"You know what I mean."

The knock increased in its intensity. Lorna motioned toward the door. "Then answer it before someone thinks I passed on during the night."

Shaking his head, Ross exited the dining room. When he opened the door, the tall bloke from the day before, who had walked with Lorna and Fergus, stood there. Ross hated having to look up to meet the dragonman's eyes, especially since the bloke was more handsome than Ross liked. "Yes?"

The dragonman looked around Ross. "Is Lorna up and about yet?"

"Who wants to know?" Ross growled out.

The man raised his brows and answered, "Ah. You must be the one she hesitated about yesterday."

The dragonman's statement made Ross wonder if Lorna had wanted him as long as Ross had wanted her. "And who the bloody hell are you?"

"Stuart MacKay of Clan Seahaven. Lorna and I are old friends. I just stopped by to see her before I leave later today. We have a lot to catch up on."

The mention of the too handsome man leaving made Ross stand a little taller. "Well, she's eating her breakfast. You'll have to come back later."

Stuart opened his mouth, but Lorna's voice boomed out before he could say anything. "Ross Anderson, he'll do no such thing."

Turning his head, Ross spotted Lorna. When she stopped next to him, she looked to Stuart and smiled. "Hello, Stu."

When Stuart smiled back, Ross clenched his fingers. The sooner he could get rid of Stuart, the sooner he could find out about the full extent of their past. Lorna had claimed they'd nearly been mated, and he wanted to know if she still had feelings for her old lover. Stuart's presence was a blatant reminder of how much he still had to learn about Lorna MacKenzie.

Lorna stepped aside, the motion causing her nightgown to show more of her figure than Ross liked. "Come in, Stu. I have enough porridge for you, too. I know it's your favorite."

Of course, it bloody was.

As Lorna guided Stuart to the kitchen, Ross took a deep breath and tried to get a grip on his jealousy. Lorna had chosen him, end of story.

And yet, his brain understood that, but his heart was being bloody stubborn. Breakfast with Lorna's "old friend" would test his patience.

Be careful, Anderson, or you might push her away. Aye, Lorna didn't like unnecessary drama. The trick would be in not becoming a third wheel to their conversation because there was no way he was leaving Lorna alone with the dragonman. Ross trusted Lorna, but given the flash of hunger and male appreciation in the dragonman's eyes a minute ago, he trusted Stuart MacKay about as far as he could throw him.

~~~

Lorna shouldn't like Ross's jealousy around Stuart, but both woman and beast rather enjoyed it.

Her dragon huffed. *I like knowing Ross would fight for us. Even if Stu challenged him to a battle, I think Ross would accept if it meant keeping us.*

Aye, I agree. Our human is more like a dragon-shifter than he knows. Maybe living on Lochguard has rubbed off on him.

Why do you say that as if it were a bad thing?

Stuart's voice interrupted Lorna's conversation with her beast. "I half expected for at least one of your children to be here. From what Fergus told me, your cottage is never empty."

80

Ross grunted. "It's not empty."

Lorna bit back a smile. "Last night was a bit special, and Faye stayed with a friend. Besides, as Ross pointed out, he's here with me."

Stuart looked to her human. "Aye, I see him." Stuart met her gaze again. "Although, I'm a bit unclear about how he lives on Lochguard since he's not a human sacrifice."

Entering the kitchen, Lorna took down another bowl for porridge. "His daughter was a sacrifice and is mated to Fraser. Finn did some negotiating, which allowed Ross to accompany his daughter. He had cancer and needed care."

From the corner of her eye, Lorna saw Ross stand tall. "It's gone now, though. I'm healthy as a horse."

Stuart chuckled. "Too bad you're not as healthy as a dragon-shifter."

Lorna sensed Ross's temper creeping up on him, so she spoke before he could. "Just because humans and dragon-shifters are different doesn't make humans any less special. You, of all people, should understand that Stu." While Stu sobered up, Lorna explained to Ross, "Stuart had a human mate."

Ross's posture relaxed at the use of "had" and he murmured, "I'm sorry for your loss."

Stuart waved a hand. "Deb will always be with me. But let's not ruin a perfectly fine breakfast by talking about dead mates. We should focus on the future we have in front of us."

After handing Stuart his porridge, she moved to stand next to Ross. She'd allowed her human to stew long enough, so she leaned against his side. "Aye, I look forward to the future."

Ross looped an arm around her waist. For a second, sadness flashed in Stuart's eyes, but it was gone before she could blink. The dragonman smiled again. "Well, my immediate future includes eating this porridge before it goes cold. Oh, and maybe embarrassing Lorna as well. I'm sure Ross would love to hear about Lorna in her youth. She was quite the firecracker."

Ross snorted. "And she still is."

Stuart exited into the dining room. Before Ross could follow, Lorna kissed Ross and whispered, "I can sit on your lap in the dining room if it eases your male pride. But just know I picked you, Ross. Stuart is just a friend, and probably a lonely one. Remember, he was exiled from Lochguard over a decade ago."

Squeezing her side, Ross answered, "Then let's try to make him feel welcome again."

"That was a quick turnaround. I'm surprised I didn't hurt my neck from the whiplash."

Ross shrugged one shoulder. "You made the claim, and that's good enough for me. Considering Lochguard dragon-shifters take honor rather seriously, at least for those who know you and call you a friend, I expect Stuart to fall into that category. Am I right?"

"Aye, you are." She kissed his cheek. "And since he can hear everything we're saying right now anyway, how about we join Stu in the dining room? Your porridge will be cold before long."

"You and the bloody porridge."

She tsked. "Complain as long as you like, but you're eating it, even if you have to cut it with a knife because you let it sit too long."

Stuart's voice drifted in from the dining room. "Aye, she'll see through her threat, too, Ross. I once had to eat cold, congealed stew because I didn't like the cooked carrots in it. Lorna all but had me chained to the table."

Lorna pushed Ross through the door as she answered, "I was raised to eat what was in front of me, whether I liked it or not. And so were you. So stop your moaning."

Her dragon spoke up again. *Liar. You always found a way to hide your broccoli and later bury it in the garden.*

Hush.

Ross pulled out a chair, and Lorna sat down as he slid it back. Once her human also sat down, Lorna picked up a spoon just as Stuart answered, "That's not what your late brother told me." Stuart looked to Ross. "Make her some broccoli and then give her the same speech."

Grinning, Ross nodded. "Aye, I just might. Maybe then she'll stop serving me this blasted porridge."

Lorna glanced at them. "If I had known you two would form a coalition against me, I would never have let Stu inside."

Ignoring her comment, Ross leaned forward and looked to Stuart. "So, what else can you tell me? I have a feeling I'm going to need a few cards to play to keep Lorna on her toes."

Stuart answered, "Well, she does have this thing about dragonflies…"

As Stuart and Ross became engrossed in the discussion of her fears and faults, Lorna couldn't help but smile. She'd known Ross was a good male, but him taking to Stuart so soon raised her esteem of him. All her human had needed to know was she wanted him and only him. After that, the past was in the past.

She wasn't sure a dragon-shifter male would've been so accepting. More and more she was starting to see the benefits to claiming a human.

She only hoped it would last.

Her dragon spoke up again. *It will. After all, I approve of Ross.*

Aye, and that's all that matters?

I'm an excellent judge of character. I was right with Jamie, and I'll be right with Ross.

I hope so, dragon. I just worry about more attacks or something else happening to take him away from me.

I won't let that happen.

While her beast merely saying that wasn't enough to make it true, the certainty in her dragon's tone did ease some of Lorna's worries.

Just as she took a bite of her breakfast, Ross met her eyes and winked. The small action made her belly flutter.

Lorna pushed aside her doubts and fears. She always fought to protect what was hers, and that now included Ross Anderson, too.

CHAPTER NINE

A few days later, Ross ended the call with his daughter and tried not to grin. Finn had granted Ross's request, which meant he could finally tell Lorna about his surprise.

He found her downstairs at the front door, saying her farewells to Meg Boyd. Ross had erred on the side of caution and let the two women talk without him. The last thing he needed was to hear about the sexual escapades of Meg and her two dragonmen.

The door clicked closed. Lorna turned her head to meet his gaze. "Came out of hiding, did you?"

Closing the distance between them, he hugged Lorna to his side. "I wasn't hiding. I'm sure you didn't want my wisearse comments interrupting you two every few minutes."

"Oh, I doubt you would've interrupted us. The tales of Meg, Archie, and Cal are quite amusing. The two dragonmen are pressuring her to choose one of them. Worse than that, they both keep threatening to destroy the other's farm unless Meg picked them."

Ross chuckled as they entered the living room. "I still say Finn should build a ten-foot wall separating their farms from the rest of the clan. That way the clan doesn't have to worry about a rogue branch or rock flying toward them."

Lorna sat down on the couch. "Why would Finn do that? Watching that pair is amusing. I've been doing it for most of my life."

Sitting down next to Lorna, Ross took her hand. "Speaking of your life, I have a surprise for you."

She studied him. "I'm not sure if I should be excited or afraid of that."

"Oh, definitely excited."

"Stop dragging it out and just tell me already. I have a long list of things to do today."

"No, you don't."

Lorna frowned. "What are you talking about?"

"You and I are going to Skye."

She blinked. "What?"

"I found out that you'd never been there and thought we could spend some time alone." Lorna opened her mouth to protest, but Ross cut her off. "It's perfectly safe. Lochguard's Protectors train there and the humans living on the island are friendly to our clan. From what I understand, they even have a sort of alliance that's held with Lochguard for centuries."

"I know that, but what I was going to say before you cut me off is that I'm helping Kaylee with her cooking this week, as well as babysitting wee Jamie two days to give Fergus and Gina some time together."

Ross put up a hand. "No, you're not. All of that is sorted. Kaylee is going to work with Meg Boyd for cooking, and Holly has agreed to watch wee Jamie in your stead. It's high time you took a holiday, Lorna." He leaned closer. "And not just any holiday, but one with me."

Under normal circumstances, Lorna would brush off Ross's cockiness. However, the thought of seeing the beauty of Skye with her human at her side made her heart rate kick up. It would be a place for her to make new memories with Ross; she and Jamie had never made it to Skye.

Her dragon chimed in. *We should go. I've always wanted to fly there.*

The reminder of Lorna flying lessened her enthusiasm. *It's been so long. I don't think I could make it that far.*

Of course we can. Besides, it gives me the chance to impress Ross.

Looking to her human, Lorna smiled. She had to admit it would be fun to watch Ross's face as she soared over the rocks and ridges of Skye.

Ross raised his brows. "Should I even ask why you have a devilish glint in your eye?"

"Devilish? No, it's more like anticipation."

"What for?" he asked slowly. "I somehow doubt it's to do with me naked in your bed since you've about worn me out over the last few days."

She lightly hit his side. "Hush, old man. You've enjoyed it as much as I."

"Then what plans do you have for me?"

Lorna smiled. "You'll just have to wait and see. When do we leave?"

He searched her eyes. "That was quick. I expected it to take more convincing to get you to go."

"A few days without my children barging in? Not to mention a chance to make memories with you and see somewhere new? Why wouldn't I want to go?"

He kissed her gently before murmuring, "You are full of surprises, love."

"You have no idea."

Chuckling, Ross answered, "I look forward to it. As for our departure, you have an hour. I'm already packed, so I'll take a nap while you do yours."

"You'll do no such thing. You can do those chores you've been putting off. I'm not about to leave the cottage in a tip."

"I still say the cottage is cleaner than I ever had back in Aberdeen." Lorna raised her brows and Ross sighed. "Fine, I'll get started. But just know my energy levels may not be at peak performance tonight."

Lorna lowered her voice as she laid her free hand on Ross's thigh. "Oh, I think you'll be fine. I have my own surprise for you."

"There's my sexy lass. Hard to believe you were shy around me at first."

He pulled her close and took her lips in a kiss. As he explored her mouth, Lorna straddled his lap.

She rocked against him, and Ross groaned. If not for the precious minutes of their holiday time ticking by, he would've taken her upstairs and made Lorna scream his name.

As it were, Faye's voice interrupted them. "I thought you two would be gone by now? The sooner you leave, the sooner you can get this weird snogging and shagging phase out of your systems."

Lorna turned her head. "Faye Cleopatra, watch your tone."

Faye sighed. "Yes, Mum. But aren't you supposed to be on holiday?"

Ross had an idea. "Aye, we are. But I have some chores that need doing, and you're going to help me. The sooner they're finished, the sooner we'll be out of your hair."

Lorna whispered, "Lazy human."

But Faye either didn't hear or pretended she didn't. "Then let's get started. Grant is supposed to come over and help me with my physical therapy and I'd rather you two be gone. Not that I don't love you, but I'm fairly certain Grant doesn't want to see my mum kissing Ross."

"And why not? He might learn something," Ross answered.

Lorna rolled her eyes and slipped off Ross's lap. "Just finish the chores. With Faye's help, I would hope for it to be spotless, but she's as bad as you when it comes to cleaning."

Faye shrugged. "Hey, as long as there's a path to walk on the floor and no mold growing anywhere, it's clean to me."

Lorna frowned. "So much for your army training straightening that out."

For a split second, Ross swore he saw sadness flicker in Faye's eyes, but it was gone in a heartbeat. He bet she missed being a full-time Protector; her wing injury last year still prevented her from reclaiming her former duties.

Wanting to distract Faye, Ross stood up and motioned toward the kitchen. "Let's start in there." He lowered his voice, not caring that Lorna could hear him anyway. "There might still be a few biscuits left."

Lorna smiled. "They're hiding in the cupboard above the sink."

Ross wanted to ask why she was giving in so easily, but he had a feeling Lorna had seen the same sadness in Faye's eyes.

He took two steps beyond Faye and said, "Then hurry up, Faye, my dear, or I'll eat all of the biscuits before you can blink."

"I think not."

With a growl, Faye charged into the kitchen. Ross chuckled, blew Lorna a kiss, and followed Faye into the other room.

~~~

An hour later, Lorna stood frowning at the edge of Lochguard's rear landing and takeoff area. "Why are you coming with us, Iris? We'll be safe enough. You should stay here."

Iris Mahajan was one of Lochguard's Protectors and their best tracker.

The golden-skinned female with long, black hair shrugged. "No matter how much you argue with me, Lorna MacKenzie, I'm not going to contradict Grant and Finn's orders. Are you ready to go?"

Lorna huffed, but Ross spoke up before she could. "Aye, we are. But could you give us a minute?"

With a nod, Iris walked to the far side and started shucking her clothes.

Ross averted his gaze to focus on Lorna. "The attack on Lochguard didn't happen that long ago, love. It's a miracle Finn is even letting us off the land. If he thinks we need an extra Protector besides the one on Skye, then I say we accept the help."

Lorna sighed. "I know. It's just hard to accept the loss of our freedom. Unlike in England, we've had the freedom to fly most anywhere in Scotland for centuries. I don't revel in the fact I have to look over my shoulder, especially given how long it's been since I flew such a great distance."

Ross cupped her cheek and searched her eyes. "I can ask Iris to carry me if it'll help."

Her dragon spoke up. *Ross won't be a burden. We're stronger than you think.*

And you're cocky. It will take half an hour to get there. The longest flight we've had in years was fifteen minutes.

And who's fault was that?

Ross's voice interrupted her conversation. "You have nothing to prove to me, Lorna MacKenzie. What was it you always told me throughout my cancer treatments and subsequent recovery?"

"A true hero knows when to ask for help," she murmured.

"Aye, so be a true hero. Should I ride with Iris?"

Lorna's pride wanted to reject the idea. "You're too clever for your own good, human."

Ross grinned. "I'm surprised you haven't admitted that before now."

Lightly slapping his arm, Lorna answered, "Your ego is going to be the death of you." Ross chuckled. Lorna smiled before glancing over at Iris standing naked on the far side of the clearing. Lorna turned Ross's back to the young dragonwoman as she said, "Stay like this while I talk to Iris."

"Is she naked then?"

"Yes, but I warn you—turn around and you'll be sleeping alone tonight."

Ross shook his head. "My jealous dragonwoman."

"Hmph," Lorna answered before striding toward Iris.

Her beast spoke up again. *I like Ross. I can't wait to play with him some more in my dragon form.*

Then you'd better behave until we reach the cottage on Skye.

As if you could stop me.

Rather than waste time arguing, Lorna focused on Iris. The dragonwoman raised her brows and asked, "What is it, Lorna?"

Lorna hesitated a second, but quickly brushed it aside. "Would you mind carrying Ross to Skye? I'm not sure I can manage it."

Surprise flashed in Iris's brown eyes, but it was quickly replaced by approval. "Of course." Iris looked to Ross's back and then back to Lorna. Amusement tinged her voice as she added, "Send him my way once I shift. I'll also hold off shifting back until after you safely take Ross away. That way he won't see me naked."

"Thanks, Iris."

"Anything for you, Lorna. You welcomed my parents with open arms when they came from India seeking shelter from the dragon wars going on there, back before I was born. It still means a lot to them."

Lorna waved a hand. "It wasn't anything special. I did what anyone would do."

Iris smiled. "If you say so." Lorna opened her mouth, but Iris cut her off. "I'll shift now. The sooner we leave, the sooner you can have your romantic holiday with your new male."

Running a few feet away, Iris stopped, and her body glowed a light purple. As Iris's arms grew into forearms and hind legs, Lorna turned back toward Ross. As soon as she was close enough, she said, "You can turn around now.

Ross pivoted around and finished with a dramatic flourish of his arms. "I didn't even peek once. I should be rewarded for that."

Rolling her eyes, Lorna pointed toward the large basket with giant iron rings in the middle of the landing area. "Just go. Iris is going to take you."

Leaning close, Ross kissed Lorna before murmuring, "There's my lass."

"Hurry up, human. The longer you linger, the longer it takes to get to Skye."

As Ross headed toward the basket not far from Iris's purple dragon, Lorna smiled to herself. She had a feeling Ross would always look out for her. Just knowing that felt…nice.

THE DRAGON'S HEART

Her dragon spoke up. *Of course it does. We should hurry up and mate him so he can't run away.*

I highly doubt Ross would run anywhere.

You know what I mean. He makes us feel beautiful, looks out for us, and helps with the children. What more could you want?

Lorna wanted love, but it was too soon to hope Ross felt that way, no matter what she might feel.

Ross had been stealing her heart for months, although Lorna had been too stubborn to realize it until the past few days. Not that she was going to admit it to her dragon.

Rather than continue the conversation with her beast, Lorna merely stated, *Let's shift.*

Finally.

After quickly taking off her clothes and storing them in the large bag she would carry in the grip of a forearm, Lorna closed her eyes. She imagined her fingers extending into talons, wings growing from her back, and her body stretching to her dragon's full height. A second later, she beat her green wings once for good measure.

Ross's booming voice caught her attention. "It's a race, love. Whoever gets there first can claim a fantasy for tonight."

Before she could do more than blink, Iris hovered in place and clutched the metal rings with her back talons. Then the purple dragon beat her wings upward and disappeared into the distance.

Crouching down, Lorna picked up her bag with her forearm and leapt into the sky. Using every bit of strength she possessed, Lorna pushed herself upward. Under normal circumstances, Lorna had no chance of beating Iris. But with the Protector carrying the basket, Ross, and most of their luggage, Lorna might have a shot. The trick would be in not getting lost. It had been many years since she'd flown to western Scotland.

Her dragon huffed. *I never get lost.*

Let's hope so, dragon. Let's hope so.

Lorna was so determined to win that her fear of something happening to her in flight, like how Jamie had died in a lightning storm, never reared its ugly head.

CHAPTER TEN

Not long after Lorna reached the edge of Skye, a twinge started in her left shoulder. Each beat of her wings intensified the pain shooting through her body.

Lorna said to her beast, *We need to land. If we keep going, we may not be able to fly for over a week.*

Her dragon huffed. *We're nearly there. A bit longer won't hurt.*

Since calling her beast stupid would be counterproductive, Lorna took another approach. *Do you want to take Ross up into the air in the next few days?*

Of course.

Another pain jarred her body. *Keep this up, and we won't be able to play with our human. A ten-minute rest will do us good. I promise not to shift back or contain you. I know how much you miss being in this form.*

Her dragon paused a few seconds before replying, *Just a few minutes. I see a good place to land ahead.*

As they descended, Lorna spotted the relatively flat piece of land nestled among hills, a stream, and lots of rocks.

After gliding down slowly, Lorna's hind legs touched the ground. No sooner had she closed her wings against her back, a human's head covered in an old, worn fedora popped up from behind a hill.

She froze. As far as she knew, there weren't any dragon hunters on Skye. But until she knew for certain who the male was, Lorna watched his every move.

The male climbed up and over the small hill in the ground. Mud covered his feet, knees, and hands. He was young, maybe her sons' age, but that was all she could tell with the hat obscuring a proper view.

He finally spoke with a southern English accent. "Hello, dragon. Fancy meeting you here."

Lorna frowned as much as a dragon could and wished she could ask him a question. But there was no way she was going to shift into her human form in front of the stranger, especially since she had sharp talons and impressive strength as long as she stayed a dragon.

The human put his hands out to his sides, palms up. "I won't hurt you. I'm more interested in what's buried over there than killing a dragon." She huffed, and the human placed his hands on his hips. "My name's Max. Excuse my muddy appearance, but that tends to happen when digging a trench."

Trench was an odd word to use for a hole. Not that Lorna cared about his word choices. Listening carefully, Lorna didn't hear anything other than the wind. The tall, lean male was here alone.

Her dragon spoke up again. *I say just scoop him up, and we can drop him in one of the sea lochs along the way to the cottage.*

We already were having trouble flying, and now you want to add extra weight? Just hush and let me think.

Her beast grunted but didn't say anything else.

Lorna's options were few. She might be able to fly long enough to get away from the human, but then she ran the risk of him telling others that there were dragons on Skye. The locals were loyal to Lochguard, but the human was English, and she didn't trust him.

The other possibility would be knocking the human unconscious and keeping him gripped in her talons until someone came to find her. Lorna was always on time so Iris would suspect something straight away when Lorna didn't show.

Max took a step toward her and Lorna tensed in case she needed to pounce. The male clicked his tongue. "Look at that. You think I'm a threat, don't you?" He chuckled as he adjusted his hat. "I'm the furthest thing from a threat, dragon. To be honest, I'm digging without permission and don't fancy being caught myself. So, if you fly away, I won't tell anyone about you and you don't tell anyone about me. Deal?"

In order to give her some time to think of what to do, Lorna bared her teeth. That should scare the human.

However, a look of wonderment filled his eyes, and he took a step forward. "So that's what they look like in a living a dragon. I've only ever seen them buried in the ground."

Growling, Lorna assessed him again. Why would he be digging up dragon teeth? Was he some sort of eccentric bone collector?

Max retreated a few steps and put up his hands again. "No need to growl at me. I'm an archaeologist and digging things up is my passion." She growled again, and he added, "My interest is dragon-shifters up through the Roman conquest of Britain. However, no one will give me a grant, let alone pay me, for that. So I pretend to look for human Iron Age and Roman settlements. They usually bring me to the right place for the dragons of that time period, too. As long as I find enough human evidence to convince people I'm doing my job properly, I can keep up this charade. Maybe you can help me convince dragon-shifters to help, too? That would be brilliant if we could set up an alliance to preserve British dragon archaeology."

Lorna blinked. What was he nattering about?

From the corner of her eye, she noticed a purple dragon approaching. It was Iris.

Wanting to keep the human from noticing her approach, she plodded closer to him and pointed to the hole in the ground.

Excitement filled Max's eyes. "That trench there should tell me if the old dragon-shifters of Skye had their base here. The references are spotty at best in historical documents, but I think I've finally figured it out."

Max's tone was so engaging that Lorna almost wanted to hear more.

Then she remembered he could be a threat for all she knew.

Thankfully, she didn't have to distract him any longer since Iris swooped down and gripped his middle in her talons. Max shouted as Iris hovered with him in place.

As Max's hat hit the ground, he glared up at Iris. "That's my favorite hat."

Confusion flashed in Iris's eyes but quickly dissipated. She met Lorna's gaze and tilted her head. She was asking if Lorna could fly away or not.

Testing out her wing, Lorna nodded to Iris. She could manage a short distance.

Jumping into the air, Lorna flapped her wings until she could glide on the wind currents. She had no idea what Iris would do with Max, but she could find that out later. Right now, Ross would be worried, and Lorna yearned to see his smiling face again.

THE DRAGON'S HEART

~~~

Ross stood next to Shay, one of Lochguard's youngest Protectors, and tried not to let worry thread his voice as he asked, "Are you sure Iris can find her? Maybe we should contact Lochguard."

Shay shook his head. "We'll wait to call anyone until Iris comes back. Otherwise, Finn will never allow his aunt off Lochguard's land again."

"I bet the bloody stubborn woman pushed herself too far too quickly. She hasn't flown much in years," Ross muttered.

Shay remained quiet for a few seconds before he replied, "She probably did it to impress you."

Looking to Shay, Ross raised his brows. "What?"

"I've known Lorna my whole life, as has much of the clan. She was never unhappy, but in the last week, she's glowed. I wasn't sure of you at first, human, but after your help in the post-attack clean-up, you showed that you're dedicated and care about Lochguard. You might just be worthy enough of Lorna MacKenzie yet." Shay grunted. "But tell anyone I said that, and I will call you a liar."

Ross tried not to smile. "One day you'll learn that having a tough image means you can care, too, lad."

Shay remained silent, and Ross went back to scanning the skies. While he was doing a good job of hiding it from the young dragonman at his side, Ross worried that Lorna's delay was his fault. What if she'd broken her wing? Or, worse, crashed and a dragon hunter had found her?

The blasted woman didn't need to try to impress him. He already wanted her more than any woman since his late wife. He'd just have to make sure to convince Lorna of that once she returned. Because, damn it, she would return. He hadn't just been given his life back to have it taken from him again. He couldn't imagine living without Lorna.

He wanted her to be his mate.

The fingers tapping against his thigh stilled. The realization had come on quite suddenly, but it was the truth. He wanted Lorna by his side for the rest of his days.

She just needed to arrive safe and sound before he could do anything.

Tapping his fingers against his thigh again, Ross squinted. There was a tiny speck in the sky. After what seemed like an eternity, he could tell the dragon was green. Since Iris was purple, it had to be Lorna.

He didn't like the way the rhythm of her wings would falter every few beats. She definitely was pushing herself too hard.

Lorna finally glided down and landed. Ross motioned to Shay. "Go inside for now. I'll shout if we need you."

To his credit, the young dragonman disappeared without a word. None too soon, either, as Lorna glowed a faint green before shrinking back into her naked human form.

Ross shrugged out of his coat as he rushed forward. "About time you showed up, love."

He placed the coat around Lorna's shoulders as she answered, "It's your fault I'm late, so don't blame me. Pushing me to race like that. My old wings couldn't take the stress."

Brushing Lorna's cheek, Ross murmured, "I'm sorry. I wasn't really thinking. I sometimes forget I'm not a lad of twenty again, out to challenge anyone who dared." He raised his voice to normal levels. "But to make it up to you, I'm going to take care of you. I saw you struggling in the sky. What hurts? Should we call a doctor?"

Lorna smiled as she patted Ross's chest. "I don't need a doctor. Although some tea and warm clothes would do."

He turned until he could loop his arm around Lorna's shoulders. "Tell me what happened. And don't gloss over the details."

His dragonwoman snorted. "And now you're ordering me about like a mate."

Ross growled. Stopping, he turned to face her. "You will be my mate if I have anything to say about it, Lorna MacKenzie."

She blinked. "Pardon?"

"You heard me the first time with your supersensitive hearing, woman. I thought something had happened to you, and it felt as if someone punched a hole in my heart. I don't want to ever feel that way again. It just means I need to take care of you and make sure you don't push yourself too hard again."

"Ross," she answered breathlessly.

"That had better be a good 'Ross' and not a warning."

Rolling her eyes, Lorna smacked his side. "Tone it down a bit, human."

"No." He caressed her cheek with his thumb. "You are my future, Lorna, and I will fight for it. The only question is, do you want the same future as me?"

~~~

After Ross's question, Lorna leaned into his caresses. Each strum of his fingers relaxed her body and eased the sore muscles of her back.

She could get used to having her human around.

Her dragon spoke up. *No need to get used to it. We will keep him.*

She wanted to agree without hesitation, but a small part of her was afraid Ross might tire of her eventually. Lorna's personality tended to wear on those who weren't strong enough to stand up to it.

Her beast grunted. *Why do you doubt him? Ross has lived with us for nearly six months. Every morning we had breakfast, and every evening we watched telly together. The only thing keeping us from being a couple was sex. But he's good at that too. I want to keep him.*

Ross's voice prevented her from replying. "Tell me your doubts, Lorna, so I can erase them."

The way he said it, with such confidence, only made Lorna lean a little closer to him. It was still sometimes hard to believe Ross was human and not a dragon-shifter.

Lorna didn't break Ross's gaze. "How are you so certain you want to spend the rest of your life with me, Ross? Tell me that first."

He nodded. "Aye, I will. But I won't let you back out from answering afterward."

"I won't try, so don't worry, human."

Placing his free hand on her hip, he pulled her gently against him. At the little thrill racing through her body at the contact, she had to focus to listen to his words. "Before I came to Lochguard and stayed with you, I was struggling to find out what to do with my life. My daughter was grown, cancer was killing me, and my wife was dead. When Holly was able to get me to Lochguard, I wondered how I would fit in. Dragons were completely different from humans, or so I thought originally."

"I hope you've changed your mind," Lorna muttered.

Ross chuckled. "You're impatient, love. Let me finish." Ross raised his brows and Lorna nodded in agreement. He continued, "Your family reminded me of my own growing up.

While my brother is now in America, as a child, he and I would play with our eight cousins during summer holidays. The Anderson family gatherings make the MacKenzie ones look tame in comparison."

"I find that hard to believe."

"It's true, love. And I'll tell you all about it later. Once I finish this, aye?" He waited for Lorna's head bob before adding, "From the first day I stayed under your roof, you didn't treat me as a stranger or an invalid. No, I was simply Ross, the stubborn-headed human. With each day that passed, I forgot I might be dying and lived in the moment. Your smile, laugh, and even frowns helped me fight against my cancer even more."

"Ross."

"Aye, that's my name. Glad you remember it." Lorna rolled her eyes, and Ross grinned. "I love your eye rrolls. I try to provoke them as often as I can."

"I know, you old fool. Are you going to finish your story?"

"I'll try, although you'll interrupt me again, I'm sure." Lorna looked at him expectantly, and he spoke again. "Aye, well, when the doctor finally told me I was healthy again, the first thought I had was to rush out and tell you the news. Not Holly, but you, Lorna. I felt guilty at first, considering everything Holly had done for me, but I eventually realized why you popped into my head first. I was already halfway in love with you, woman. And when I had my life back again, I wanted to make sure you never left my side."

Lorna tilted her head. "But you never said anything."

"I didn't feel as if I had the right. Until we watched that human bloke mate the Stonefire dragonwoman, I didn't think we had a chance. Sure, we could've lived together until we were older and grayer, but I know how important matings are to dragon-shifters. I didn't want everyone to gossip, and you lose any of the respect you have with the clan."

"Ross Anderson, you are an old fool."

He frowned. "I'm trying to spill my heart out to you, and you call me a fool. Maybe I've been dreaming all this time."

"Stop joking for a minute and be serious. I've been dreaming about you for several months, too."

"Then why didn't you do anything, love? A hint would've been nice."

She ignored his joke. If she didn't get the truth out soon, she might put it off. "I'm a bit old-fashioned, aye? I know the lasses chase the lads these days, but in my time, it was rarely done. Female dragon-shifters are rare, and the males used to have to compete to woo their hearts and claim them as a mate. Add that to not wanting to let go of my Jamie, and I used both excuses as a wall around my heart. I believed it would make my life easier to keep my distance from love."

"And now?"

"And now, I'm grateful for my excuses and my wall because it meant I waited for you, Ross."

"Lorna," he rasped out before taking her lips.

He slipped his tongue between her lips and pulled her tighter against him. With each stroke of his tongue, she forgot about the pain in her back and all of the time wasted between the pair of them. She had a male she cared for in front of her, and she was going to make sure he knew how much he meant to her.

Because despite her excuses and her unwillingness to believe it could happen so quickly, she loved Ross and she wasn't going to allow anything apart from death to take him away from her. And even then, she might find a way to bring him back and scold him for leaving her.

Her dragon snarled. *Don't think about death. Kiss him and get him inside. I want sex. Now.*

For once, Lorna didn't argue with her dragon. Breaking the kiss, she whispered, "Let's go inside. I want you to make love to me."

"You don't have to ask me twice."

After one last kiss, Ross took her hand and tugged her toward the cottage. The second they were inside, Shay appeared. One look at Lorna and Ross, and he motioned toward the door. "I'll be outside."

"Go farther," Lorna hissed. She didn't want him to hear her and her human.

"No, Lorna. I'm here to protect you, and that's what I'm going to do," Shay stated.

Ross spoke up. "He'll do the right thing and pretend not to listen. Won't you, lad?"

"Aye. Believe me, the last thing I want to hear is Aunt Lorna having sex. It's as bad as hearing my own parents."

She opened her mouth to scold Shay, but he was out the door in the next second. Ross murmured, "Forget him," before nibbling her earlobe. "Show me where the bedroom is."

Yes, show him or I'll take control, her dragon said.

There was no way she was going to allow her dragon to steal this moment from her, so Lorna motioned up the stair. "Up here."

As she guided her male up the stairs, her heart thudded in her chest. She might have had sex with Ross several times over, but this time would be different.

Lorna was about to share her body with the man she loved.

CHAPTER ELEVEN

Ross and Lorna didn't waste time shedding their clothes. The instant his dragonwoman was naked, Ross laid her down on the bed. Hitching her leg around his waist, he pressed his groin against her swollen folds. Lorna moaned at the contact.

Leaning down to nip her shoulder, Ross murmured, "Foreplay will have to wait. I want to claim my mate and the woman I love."

Lorna's breath hitched. "What are you talking about?"

Cupping her cheek, Ross answered, "You heard me. I love you, Lorna MacKenzie. I suspect I have for months now, although I always found a way to deny it. As soon as we get back to Lochguard, we're going to find a way to have a mating ceremony. Even if it means I have to bloody stand up in front of cameras for some PR stunt."

She smiled. "Do I get a say in this?"

"In hypotheticals, aye. In real life, no."

She laughed at the reversal of her own words earlier in the week. Damn, had it only been that long?

Lorna's hand reached between them and gripped his cock. All thoughts left his head at her touch.

His dragonwoman whispered, "I love you, too, Ross Anderson. Now show me how much you love me."

Running his hand down her cheek, her neck, and finally to her breast, he answered, "I can't do much while you grip my cock." He took her nipple and rolled it between his fingers. The sight of Lorna closing her eyes and throwing back her head only sent more blood to his cock.

She finally released him and gripped his shoulders. He ordered, "Look at me." As soon as Lorna opened her eyes and met his gaze, he added, "I want to watch your beautiful eyes as you come apart in my arms, love."

"Ross."

Rather than answer, Ross thrust into her wet heat. Lorna dug her nails into his skin, and he moved his hips. "You're mine, Lorna MacKenzie. And I'm going to claim you properly."

Gripping her leg around his waist, Ross ran his hand down to her arse cheek. He took a possessive grip as he increased his pace. "My beautiful dragonwoman. Tell me again you love me."

"I love you, Ross." Lorna moaned as he circled his hips. "And not just because you're good in bed."

"If you think this is good, you haven't seen anything yet."

Lorna opened her mouth, but Ross brushed the bundle of nerves between her thighs. As he increased the pressure, Lorna bit her lip and struggled to keep from closing her eyes.

He was glad she didn't because the love and desire burning in them only pushed him to move faster.

"Yes, just like that," Lorna said in a husky voice.

"Tell me what you want, love. I aim to please my woman."

Lightly scratching his back, Lorna replied, "I want you as you are, Ross. No more, no less."

"Damn, I love you, Lorna." He took her lips in a rough kiss. The combined heat of her mouth on his and her core around his cock pushed him closer to the edge. If he weren't careful, he'd come before Lorna. No dragon-shifter would allow that, and neither would he.

Increasing the pressure against her hard little nub, Lorna groaned, and the vibration shot down his spine. Breaking the kiss, he growled out, "I love you," before pressing harder. Lorna screamed his name as she gripped and released his cock.

Then he gave one last thrust and stilled as he shouted Lorna's name. Pleasure coursed through his body as he came inside her.

With one last shudder, Ross collapsed on top of her. Her arms instantly came around his back and hugged him tightly.

Taking a deep inhalation of her scent, Ross sighed. "This is heaven."

"For once, I'm not going to disagree with you."

Rather than make a quip, he grunted and rolled to his side, never letting go of Lorna. He kissed her cheek and said, "Are you okay, love? I know you hurt yourself flying here."

Snuggling into his side, Lorna answered, "I'll have a twinge in my upper back for a day or two, but nothing to worry about. That gives you a few days to truly impress me with your skills. If you don't, then I'm going to let my dragon out to play."

"And what does that entail? I'm almost afraid to ask."

"Let's just say you won't be able to walk properly for days. She's quite the lusty thing."

"Considering we have a precious few days alone, I don't want to spend it with ice over my crotch if I can help it." He nuzzled her cheek with his. "But first, I want to cuddle my woman for a while."

He tightened his arms around her, and Lorna kissed his chest. "That, combined with peace and quiet, sounds like my idea of paradise."

The Dragon's Heart

As they lay in comfortable silence, Ross felt more content than he had in a long time. Not even the thought of telling Lorna's children about their desire to mate would ruin the moment.

~~~

Lorna listened to Ross's heartbeat. The steady rhythm, combined with his strong arms around her, was slowly lulling her asleep.

Her dragon spoke up. *Not yet. We only had one orgasm. I want more.*

Hush, dragon. We have the rest of our lives to do that. Right now, however, I want to lie here with Ross's arms around us. It's been too long since I had this kind of closeness.

She half expected her beast to say it was Lorna's fault, but she merely settled down at the back of her mind and remained silent.

As Lorna struggled to keep her eyes open, Ross's voice caught her attention. "Do you think the clan will accept us?"

Lifting her head a fraction, she looked up at her human. "Of course they will."

"You sound so confident, love."

"Ross, I'm not a naïve young female who thinks everyone will toss rose petals and wish us luck. But most of the clan looks to me for advice. If I approve of you, they will, too."

"I suppose since even Fraser came around, I shouldn't worry too much."

She smiled. "I wouldn't hold my breath on that truce being permanent. Fraser will always be protective of me, as are all of my children. Holly is probably the same."

"Aye, she is. She might be more levelheaded than Fraser, but she's brave. When she was a child, she always stood up to those who bullied the weaker in her classes. She didn't care if it alienated her from the popular students; she wanted to do what was right."

Lorna laid her head on Ross's chest again. "Hearing that, it's only logical she would join the sacrifice program to save you."

"Aye, although I still worry about her. In some ways, I'm glad she has Fraser. He'll protect her from her greatest enemy—her big heart and determination to save everyone." He stroked her back. "Just like I'm going to have to do the same with you, Lorna."

She wouldn't try to deny it. "Good, because I don't have as much energy as I once did and helping anyone who asks for it is a bit tiring."

Ross chuckled. "I may need to implement an appointment system where you're only available a certain amount of hours a week."

"I'm not so sure about that. I have five more grandchildren coming, and I'm going to spoil all of them as much as I like."

"Okay, we'll put in exceptions for grandkids. But for everyone else, maybe only five or eight hours a week? You're sixty, after all."

Lorna snorted. "Make me sound ancient while you're at it."

He rubbed her back in long strokes, and Lorna's dragon hummed inside her mind. "Ninety might be ancient. Sixty is more like you're discovering yourself all over again. We just need to get Faye out of the house, first, though. Just in case rediscovering yourself involves naked dancing."

She tickled his side, and Ross laughed. When she finally stilled her fingers, she moved to straddle his legs with her own.

Bracing herself on his chest with her hands, Lorna said, "If I'm naked, then I'm not going to be dancing. Well, unless it's between the sheets."

Ross groaned. "Did you really just say that?"

Lorna grin. "Aye. It looks as if your corniness is rubbing off on me."

"What did you say? All I heard was 'rubbing' and wondered why you weren't doing it."

Lightly smacking his chest, she wiggled her hips to torture her human. Ross drew in a breath, and she did it again. "I wasn't sure if it was your nap time or not. You seemed fairly adamant about slowing down."

Ross placed his hands on her hips possessively. "That might have been true earlier, but you must have some special dragon-shifter recharging abilities because I might just break our record to date. Three orgasms in a row should do it." He lowered his voice and huskiness sent shivers down her spine. "And one of them will come from my tongue."

As she stared into Ross's brown eyes, all she saw was love, heat, and a dash of playfulness. Even if Ross were eighty, she imagined he'd never stop looking at her like that.

Her dragon spoke up. *Of course not. Our heated looks will drive him mad for the rest of his days.*

Lorna didn't disagree with her beast.

Brushing a hand through his gray chest hair, she murmured, "I love you, cockiness and all."

"It's not cockiness if it's the truth." She shook her head, but Ross spoke again before she could. "And you'd better get used to it, Lorna MacKenzie, because I love you and am never letting you go."

Lorna lifted her hips and Ross positioned his cock between them. As she sunk down, both dragon and woman felt complete in a way they hadn't in nearly thirty years. Maybe if she'd been twenty years younger and of childbearing age, Ross might've stirred the mate-claim frenzy.

But true mate or not, Ross Anderson was hers to keep. The only trick would be in finding a way to mate the man she loved in front of the clan. Her human didn't deserve anything less.

Then Ross guided her hips back and forth, and Lorna forgot about everything except the male inside her.

EPILOGUE

One month later

Lorna adjusted the dark blue shoulder strap of her traditional dress for the tenth time. The blasted thing kept slipping. "I should've brought some tape."

Faye rolled her eyes. "Right, because that's what every dragon-shifter brings to her mating ceremony."

Lorna tsked. "I thought you agreed to be somewhat less sarcastic today."

"Aye, I'm trying. It's quite difficult, though."

Fraser peeked his head inside the small room. "Aren't you ready yet, Mum? The great hall still doesn't have a roof and the tents only keep out so much of the drizzle."

Lorna raised an eyebrow. "I don't recall you having such trouble with rain when you snuck out as a young lad."

"Aye, well, it's Holly I'm worried about, not me. She shouldn't be out in the chill," Fraser answered.

Faye shook her head. "Holly is wearing at least three layers plus a jacket. She'll be fine."

"I still don't like it," Fraser muttered.

Lorna stood tall. "I'm just glad you haven't decided to sabotage the ceremony. You and Ross were gone a long time last night. I wasn't sure if you had tried to carry him back to Aberdeen or not."

Fraser put on a look of mock shock. "You think so little of me, Mother."

Despite herself, Lorna smiled. "Aye, with good reason."

Faye moved to the door. "Come, Fraser. The longer you stand here chatting, the longer Holly is out in the cold. If you're so determined to get your mate inside, then let's go."

Fergus's head appeared next to Fraser's. "Aye, let's go. Holly sent me to retrieve you. She thought you might be trying to kidnap Mum."

Fraser sighed. "Even my mate is against me. I'm not sure how I'll keep on going now."

Fergus placed a hand on Fraser's shoulder. "You can wax on about your dire circumstances later. Come on."

As Fergus guided Fraser away, Faye turned to face Lorna. "I was going to wait until later, but I have an early mating present for you."

"Aye?"

"I'm getting my own cottage."

Lorna closed the space between them and searched her daughter's eyes. "Is this what you want? I don't wish for you to move out just on my account."

Faye smiled. "Mum, you've taken care of me long enough. You and Ross will want some privacy, and I need to focus on finding my new place in the clan."

She touched Faye's cheek. "Don't give up on your dream, hen."

Faye placed her hand over Lorna's. "I won't, Mum. But no amount of physical therapy will get me back to where I once was. I need to accept that."

"Whatever you do, I'll be there for you, Faye."

Faye blinked, probably to keep back tears. "I know, Mum." Her daughter cleared her throat. "But enough about me. Ross is probably starting to wonder where you are. And at his age, you don't want to get his blood pressure up."

"He's not that old, Faye Cleopatra." Faye grinned, and Lorna's love for her daughter spread throughout her body. "I love you, hen."

"Love you, too, Mum." Faye walked to the door. "I'll let them know you're coming!"

With that, Faye left Lorna alone. The thought of an empty cottage would've crushed Lorna a few months ago, but now she had Ross. The sooner she mated him, the sooner she would have someone by her side for the rest of her life.

Her dragon grunted. *Why are we still standing here? Let's go. The sooner we get your human celebrations out of the way, the sooner I can claim Ross tonight.*

You just had him last night.

Aye, but I want more.

Pushing aside her beast's lusty thoughts, Lorna exited the small room that hadn't been damaged in the attack and walked down the hall. At the entrance to what had once been the great hall, she took a deep breath and entered the room.

Clan members filled the spaces between the former walls of the room. By the look of things, the entire clan had turned out for her mating ceremony.

However, after a cursory glance, Lorna met Ross's gaze, and everyone else melted away at his wink. Even after all this time, one wink sent shivers down her spine.

Wanting to put a formal claim on him, Lorna picked up her pace. It was time to take Ross Anderson as her mate.

~~~

While Ross was grateful he and Lorna's ceremony wasn't being broadcasted, the front row of photographers from both media outlets and the Department of Dragon Affairs irritated him a wee bit more with each click and flash of the camera. At this rate, his vision would be full of spots, and he wouldn't be able to appreciate Lorna's beauty.

Then he finally saw her enter the room. The dark blue of the dress made her skin glow, but he barely noticed as he held her gaze. Every day he wondered how he was lucky enough to have Lorna MacKenzie at his side, let alone her love, too.

But for whatever reason, he did, and Ross was less than five minutes away from claiming Lorna as his mate for the rest of their lives.

At that thought, he realized he would gladly brave a hundred cameras and go permanently blind if it meant securing the DDA's permission again to mate his woman.

Luckily, he already possessed the signed document in his sporran. His and Lorna's mating was legal.

Lorna walked toward him, never taking her gaze from him. When she finally arrived at his side, he took her hands and squeezed. Not caring that every dragon-shifter in the room could hear him, he murmured, "You're so lovely."

"You clean up well yourself."

There had been some debate, but ultimately, Ross had convinced Lorna to let him wear the human kilt with the Anderson tartan of blue, red, and yellow, paired with a black suit jacket and bowtie.

The Dragon's Heart

They probably would've gone on staring at each other for a while if Finn hadn't cleared his throat from the front row. No doubt, he was worried about Arabella.

Sometimes, Ross wondered how female dragon-shifters kept from murdering their mates in their sleep.

Releasing Lorna's hands, Ross picked up the silver arm cuff engraved with his name in the old language. "Lorna Stewart MacKenzie, before everyone here today, I claim you as my mate. I never thought I'd get a second chance in my lifetime, but you were the shining star in a sea of darkness. Through your sheer stubbornness, you kept me from dying. I fought cancer and won for you, love. Please tell me you'll accept my mate claim."

"Of course I will, despite your hyperbole."

Grinning, Ross placed the cuff on Lorna's upper arm. Seeing the silver glinting in the light and knowing it was his name on her arm satisfied a primal part of him.

Lorna picked up a silver ring engraved with her name in the old language. The clever dragonwoman had suggested incorporating both human and dragon-shifter traditions into the ceremony, to show the dragons were open to new ways of doing things, too.

If he could love her more, Ross would.

Lorna eased the ring on the fourth finger of his left hand. "I accept your claim, Ross Anderson. Everything about you makes my life more fulfilling. I never expected to laugh or love as hard as I once had. But then you showed up in my life, and my heart woke up. Not only do I shiver at your touch, but I also love how you care for others, including me. You will keep me on my toes for the rest of my life, and I look forward to the adventure. I love you, Ross, and claim you as mine in front of the entire clan."

"Good, then come here."

As the audience chuckled, Ross pulled Lorna flush against his body and kissed her. Each stroke of her tongue against his made him forget about everyone watching them. At that moment, all he could think about was the dragonwoman who had stolen his heart and given him a second chance at a happily ever after.

Dear Reader:

I hope you enjoyed Ross and Lorna's story. Their story was a lot more fun to write than I had anticipated! The Lochguard dragons are always a hoot and I hope you continue to follow the clan. ☺

Also, if you haven't yet read my other dragon series, about the Stonefire Dragons, then what are you waiting for? You can check out the first book, *Sacrificed to the Dragon*, which is available in paperback.

Oh, and if you have a chance, would you leave a review? It would help me out a lot.

Thanks so much for reading and turn the page to enjoy an excerpt from one of my other series.

With Gratitude,
Jessie Donovan

Blaze of Secrets
(Asylums for Magical Threats #1)

After discovering she has elemental fire magic as a teenager, Kiarra Melini spends the next fifteen years inside a magical prison. While there, she undergoes a series of experiments that lead to a dangerous secret. If she lives, all magic will be destroyed. If she dies, magic has a chance to survive. Just as she makes her choice, a strange man breaks into cell, throws her over his shoulder, and carries her right out of the prison.

To rescue his brother, Jaxton Ward barters with his boss to rescue one other inmate--a woman he's never met before. His job is to get in, nab her and his brother, and get out. However, once he returns to his safe house, his boss has other ideas. Jaxton is ordered to train the woman and help her become part of the anti-magical prison organization he belongs to.

Working together, Kiarra and Jaxton discover a secret much bigger than their growing attraction to each other. Can they evade the prison retrieval team long enough to help save magic? Or, will they take Kiarra back to prison and end any chance of happiness for them both?

Excerpt from *Blaze of Secrets*:

CHAPTER ONE

First-born Feiru *children are dangerous. At the age of magical maturity they will permanently move into compounds established for both their and the public's protection. These compounds will be known as the Asylums for Magical Threats (hereafter abbreviated as "AMT").*
—Addendum, Article III of the *Feiru* Five Laws, July 1953

Present Day

Jaxton Ward kept his gaze focused on the nearing mountain ledge ahead of him. If he looked down at the chasm below his feet, he might feel sick, and since his current mission was quite possibly the most important one of his life, he needed to focus all of his energy on succeeding.

After all, if things went according to plan, Jaxton would finally see his brother again.

He and his team of three men were balanced on a sheet of rock five thousand feet in the air. To a human, it would look like they were flying. However, any *Feiru* would know they were traveling via elemental wind magic.

Darius, the elemental wind first-born on his team, guided them the final few feet to the mountain ledge. As soon as the sheet of rock touched solid ground, Jaxton and his team moved into position.

The mountain under their feet was actually one of the most secure AMT compounds in the world. Getting in was going to be difficult, but getting out was going to take a bloody miracle, especially since he'd had to barter with his boss for the location of his brother. In exchange, he had promised to rescue not just Garrett, but one other unknown first-born as well.

Taka, the elemental earth first-born of Jaxton's team, signaled he was ready. He nodded for Taka to begin.

As Taka reached a hand to the north, the direction of elemental earth magic, the solid rock of the mountain moved. With each inch that cleared to form a tunnel, Jaxton's heart rate kicked up. Jaxton was the reason his brother had been imprisoned inside the mountain for the last five years and he wasn"t sure if his brother had ever forgiven him.

Even if they survived the insurmountable odds, located Garrett, and broke into his prison cell, his brother might not agree to go with them. Considering the rumors of hellish treatment inside the AMT compounds, his brother's hatred would be justified.

Once the tunnel was big enough for them to enter, Jaxton pushed aside his doubts. No matter what his brother might think of him, Jaxton would rescue him, even it if took drugging Garrett unconscious to do so.

Taking out his Glock, he flicked off the safety. Jaxton was the only one on the team without elemental magic, but he could take care of himself.

He moved to the entrance of the tunnel, looked over his shoulder at his men, and nodded. After each man nodded, signaling they were ready, he took out his pocket flashlight, switched it on, and jogged down the smooth tunnel that would lead them to the inner corridors of the AMT compound.

If his information was correct, the AMT staff would be attending a site-wide meeting for the next hour. That gave Jaxton and his team a short window of opportunity to get in, nab the two inmates, and get back out again.

He only hoped everything went according to plan.

~~*

Kiarra Melini stared at the small homemade shiv in her hand and wondered for the thousandth time if she could go through with it.

She had spent the last few weeks racking her brain, trying to come up with an alternative plan to save the other prisoners of the AMT without having to harm anyone. Yet despite her best efforts, she'd come up empty-handed.

To protect the lives of the other first-borns inside the AMT, Kiarra would kill for the first and last time.

Not that she wanted to do it, given the choice. But after overhearing a conversation between two AMT researchers a few weeks ago, she knew the AMT would never again be safe for any of the first-borns while she remained alive.

The outside world might have chosen to forget about the existence of the first-born prisoners, but that didn't make them any less important. Kiarra was the only one who cared, and she would go down fighting trying to protect them.

Even if it meant killing herself to do so.

She took a deep breath and gripped the handle of her blade tighter until the plastic of the old hairbrush dug into her skin. Just as she was about to raise her arm to strike, her body shook. Kiarra closed her eyes and breathed in and out until she calmed down enough to stop shaking. Ending her life, noble as her reasons may be, was a lot harder than she'd imagined.

Mostly because she was afraid to die.

But her window of opportunity was closing fast; the AMT-wide meeting would end in less than an hour. After that, she would have to wait a whole other month before she could try again, and who knew how many more first-borns would suffer because of her cowardice.

Maybe, if she recalled the conversation between the two researchers, the one which forebode the future harsh realities of the other AMT prisoners, she'd muster enough nerve to do what needed to be done.

It was worth a shot, so Kiarra closed her eyes and recalled the conversation that had changed the course of her life forever.

Strapped to a cold metal examination table, Kiarra kept her eyes closed and forced herself to stay preternaturally still. The slightest movement would alert the researchers in the room that she was conscious again. She couldn't let that happen, not if she wanted to find out the reason why the researchers had increased her examination visits and blood draws over the past two weeks.

Most AMT prisoners wouldn't think twice about it, since they'd been conditioned not to ask questions, but Kiarra had gone through something similar before. The last time her visits had increased with the same frequency, the AMT researchers had stolen her elemental magic.

Since then, no matter how many times she reached to the south—the direction of elemental fire—she felt nothing. No tingling warmth, no comforting flame. She was no different from a non-first-born, yet she was still a prisoner, unable to see the sky or feel a breeze, and forced to live in constant fear of what the guards or researchers might do to her.

Of how they might punish her.

The Dragon's Heart

Dark memories invaded her mind. However, when the female researcher in the room spoke again, it snapped Kiarra back to the present. The woman's words might tell her more about her future, provided she had one after her treatment.

She listened with every cell in her body and steeled herself not to react.

"Interesting," the female researcher said. "Out of the ten teenagers, nine of them still can't use their elemental magic, just like F-839. Dr. Adams was right—her blood was the key to getting the Null Formula to work."

It took all of Kiarra's control not to draw in a breath. Her serial number was F-839, and all of the extra blood draws finally made sense—the AMT was using her blood to try and eradicate elemental magic.

The male researcher spoke up. "They're going to start a new, larger test group in a few weeks and see if they can stop the first-borns from going insane and/or committing suicide. If we don't get the insanity rate below ten percent, then we'll never be able to implement this planet-wide."

"Don't worry, we'll get there. We have a few million first-borns to burn through to get it right."

Kiarra opened her eyes and embraced the guilt she felt every time she thought about what had happened to those poor first-born teenagers.

Because of her blood, not only had five teenagers already gone insane, but their insanity was driving an untold number of them to suicide.

And the researchers wanted to repeat the process with a larger group.

She couldn't let that happen.

They needed her blood, drawn and injected within hours, as a type of catalyst for the Null Formula to work. If they didn't have access to her blood, they wouldn't be able to conduct any more tests.

There was a chance the researchers might find another catalyst within a few weeks or months, but it was a risk she was willing to take. Stopping the tests, even for a few months, would prevent more people from going insane or committing suicide.

Kiarra needed to die.

I can do this. Think of the others. Taking a deep breath, she tightened her grip around the shiv's handle and whispered, "Please let this work,'" before raising the blade with a steady hand and plunging it into the top half of her forearm.

Kiarra sucked in a breath as a searing pain shot up her arm. To prevent herself from making any more noise, she bit her lip. Despite the AMT-wide staff meeting, a guard would come to investigate her cell if she screamed.

You can do this, Kiarra. Finish it. With her next inhalation, she pulled the blade a fraction more down toward her wrist. This time she bit her lip hard enough she could taste iron on her tongue.

While her brain screamed for her to stop, she ignored it and gripped the handle of the blade until it bit into her palm. Only when her heart stopped beating would the other first-borns be safe—at least from her.

An image of a little girl crying, reaching out her arms and screaming Kiarra's name, came unbidden into her mind, but she forced it aside. Her sister had abandoned her, just like the rest of her family. Her death wouldn't cause anyone sadness or pain. Rather, through death, she would finally have a purpose.

This was it. On the next inhalation, she moved the blade a fraction. But before she could finish the job, the door of her cell slid open.

Kiarra looked up and saw a tall man, dressed head to toe in black, standing in her doorway and pointing a gun straight at her.

Shit. She'd been discovered.

THE DRAGON'S HEART

Want to read the rest?
Blaze of Secrets is available in paperback.

For exclusive content and updates, sign up for my newsletter at:

http://www.jessiedonovan.com

Author's Note

Originally, I hadn't planned on writing Lorna's story. But as more and more of my readers asked for her tale, I started to get the idea for this novella. Since writing about an older couple is actually risky in romance, I hope my readers enjoyed this story. In the end, I think Lorna and Ross are a perfect match for each other!

There will be about eight months between the release of this novella and the next Lochguard Highland Dragons story (about Faye and Grant). This is because I slow down a little over the summer and won't have time to write it. However, there will be a Stonefire Dragons novel released in the interim, which I hope you'll enjoy.

As ever, I thank not only my readers but also the people who help make this book a reality:

- Clarissa Yeo of Yocla Designs does all of my covers and manages to wow me each and every time!
- Becky Johnson of Hot Tree Editing is amazing and I can't imagine working with someone else. Not only does she get me, she never hesitates to point out when I need to change something.
- My beta readers, Donna H., Iliana G., and Alyson S. are also vital to the process. Not only do they catch the lingering typos, they also point out the smaller details only a dedicated fan could spot.

I hope you enjoyed Ross and Lorna's story and I look forward to writing many crazy Lochguard stories in the future. Until next time, happy reading!

ABOUT THE AUTHOR

Jessie Donovan wrote her first story at age five, and after discovering *The Dragonriders of Pern* series by Anne McCaffrey in junior high, she realized people actually wanted to read stories like those floating around inside her head. From there on out, she was determined to tap into her over-active imagination and write a book someday.

After living abroad for five years and earning degrees in Japanese, Anthropology, and Secondary Education, she buckled down and finally wrote her first full-length book. While that story will never see the light of day, it laid the world-building groundwork of what would become her debut paranormal romance, *Blaze of Secrets*.

Jessie loves to interact with readers, and when not traipsing around some foreign country on a shoestring, can often be found on Facebook. Check out her page below:

http://www.facebook.com/JessieDonovanAuthor

And don't forget to sign-up for her newsletter to receive sneak peeks and inside information. You can sign-up on her website:

http:///www.jessiedonovan.com